Praise for *Coffee & Kung Fu*

"[A] wonderful debut . . . charming, witty, and soulful. Readers will delight in the tale of one woman's journey from humorous, melancholic, lonely girl—to confident, self-knowing, young woman."

—Jill A. Davis, author of *Girls' Poker Night*

"Thanks to breezy first-person narrative, snappy dialogue, and characters so real you expect to run into them at Starbucks, newcomer Brichoux's literary debut is as vivid as her heroine's close-cropped, bright red hair. A fast-paced, hilarious, yet poignant read—if you liked *The Nanny Diaries*, you'll love *Coffee & Kung Fu!*"

—Wendy Markham, author of *Slightly Single*

"*Coffee & Kung Fu* is fresh, lively writing. One of the best parts is its use of metaphor and the elements of folklore gleaned from the Kung Fu universe. After reading Brichoux's debut you might feel, as I do, that you have not given Jackie Chan his due." —*St. Petersburg Times*

"Absolutely fabulous! A fresh, funny novel about being your own woman. Made me want to run out and rent a Kung Fu movie!"

—Melissa Senate, author of *See Jane Date*

continued . . .

"With its witty, wonderful prose and a heroine worth rooting for, *Coffee & Kung Fu* is ushering in a new trend in the chick lit genre: edgy without setting your teeth on edge. Be sure to pop it in your beach bag this summer!"

—Dangerously Curvy Novels (www.curvynovels.com)

"Who knew [Jackie Chan films] were so deep? A fun and quick read from a first-time author, this is perfect for a day at the beach."

—*Library Journal*

"A refreshing take on an increasingly crowded genre." —*Booklist*

"A young woman's guide to life—as seen through classic Jackie Chan films. Newcomer Karen Brichoux scores a coup by venturing into the cliché-strewn, warmed-over waters of Gen-X chick-lit and coming up with a bright, fresh, exciting spin on the genre. . . . Warm, smart and original: a swift Snake in Eagle's Shadow kick to all the *Bridget Jones* clones." —*Kirkus Reviews*

"Clever and heartfelt turns of phrase . . . *Coffee & Kung Fu* is an easy read, well-suited for long weekends or extended beach breaks."

—*Women's Review of Books*

Other Books by Karen Brichoux

Coffee & Kung Fu

Separation Anxiety

Karen Brichoux

New American Library

New American Library
Published by New American Library, a division of
Penguin Group (USA) Inc., 375 Hudson Street,
New York, New York 10014, U.S.A.
Penguin Books Ltd, 80 Strand,
London WC2R 0RL, England
Penguin Books Australia Ltd, 250 Camberwell Road,
Camberwell, Victoria 3124, Australia
Penguin Books Canada Ltd, 10 Alcorn Avenue,
Toronto, Ontario, Canada M4V 3B2
Penguin Books (N.Z.) Ltd, Cnr Rosedale and Airborne Roads,
Albany, Auckland 1310, New Zealand

Penguin Books Ltd, Registered Offices: 80 Strand, London WC2R 0RL, England

First published by New American Library, a division of Penguin Group (USA) Inc.

First Printing, June 2004
10 9 8 7 6 5 4 3 2 1

Ⓡ REGISTERED TRADEMARK—MARCA REGISTRADA

LIBRARY OF CONGRESS CATALOGING-IN-PUBLICATION DATA:

Brichoux, Karen.
    Separation anxiety / Karen Brichoux.
        p. cm.
    ISBN 0-451-21199-5
    1. Women museum curators—Fiction. 2. Separation (Psychology)—Fiction. 3. Chicago
(Ill.)—Fiction. 4. Friendship—Fiction. I. Title.
PS3602.R5S47 2004
    813'.6—dc22

                                                                                    2003025670

Set in Garamond Book
Designed by Erin Benach

Printed in the United States of America

For starlings everywhere

Acknowledgments

Thanking people is useless, because a simple "thanks" can never encompass the nudge here, the frown there, the laughter, the commiseration, the little things that make a friend a friend. But I'll try anyway. Thank you to BJ Robbins and Ellen Edwards for all their expertise. Thank you to Jerri Corgiat—fellow writer and fellow victim of synchronicity—for damn near everything. Thank you to Jade for walking across my keyboard and teaching me patience and for being there when I was lonely . . . and when I wasn't. Thank you to Mark Knopfler, may he always make the ordinary extraordinary. And to Dave, a big thank-you for everything and more, but most of all for introducing me to *Alchemy* a thousand years ago, and for the memory of staggering around to our own (bad) rendition of "Two Young Lovers." Sanity is overrated.

Chapter 1

"Mom says starlings are just like people," I tell Jonah as I lean back and rest my elbows on the rough wooden back of the park bench. "They're greedy, they fight all the time, and they're always together."

Jonah tosses the last of his crumbled-up hot dog bun onto the ground. Starlings rush forward, screeching, squealing, and pecking at the bread and each other. "I like starlings," he says. "They remind me of you."

I open my mouth, but he beats me to it.

"I mean, you and me. We're always together and we're always fighting." He laughs.

I laugh, too, but I know something has changed. Not with us. Not in him. In me.

I don't like starlings.

It's early spring in Chicago, and they don't call it the Windy City for laughs. The March breezes are invisible demons intent on ripping the bricks from the buildings and the warm air from your lungs. Entire newspapers cartwheel past us as we walk back to the museum—to work. I wrap my scarf over the lower half of my face and pull my hat down around my ears. It's too cold to talk. I wouldn't know what to say if we could. You can break up with a boyfriend. You can divorce a husband. But there's no official way to end a friendship. You just have to drift apart.

• • •

I was six when I first met Jonah. The first day of first grade.

"Wichita Gray?" the teacher yelled over the crowd. She pronounced it *Whi-chi-taw.*

I scuffed my toes into the gritty blue-green carpet. "Wi-*chee*-ta," I said.

I hated being the only child with a city for a name. A city everyone correctly pronounced incorrectly. Mom's priest—her current religious affiliation was Catholic—had told me God would answer all my prayers. Every night, I prayed for a name change.

But after months and months, I figured God wasn't listening.

"What? I can't hear you." The teacher cupped her hand around her ear. "People, hush. You're so squirrelly."

"Wi-*chee*-ta," I said again, my voice loud in the silence.

Someone giggled.

"Oh," the teacher said. "How nice. That's the original Indian name, you know."

I shook my head.

"We'll have to look that up," she said. "I'm sure everyone would be interested."

Everyone might be, but I didn't think so. I knew I wasn't. I just wanted to fade away.

But I survived my first day, even without fading. Survived until the organized hell euphemistically called the after-lunch recess.

"Wi-chi-taw wears a bra," Berkeley chanted. Berkeley was in my Sunday school class at church and thought he was a genius because he could rhyme. He ended the singsong taunt by trying to pinch my chest.

I took off running. And ran all the way to the monkey bars. Closing my eyes, I climbed up and swung from bar to bar, praying for a new name with each rung.

"Cheetah," said the voice of God. But the priest had never said anything about God sounding like a first grader. More like thunder and lightning. Or sneaking around at night and calling people's names twice. "Samuel, Samuel." That kind of thing.

I opened my eyes. Down under my feet was a boy from the desk group next to mine. I recognized him because he was missing both front teeth and his hair hung down over his eyes.

"You're fast," he said. "Like a cheetah. That's probably why you're named Wi-cheetah."

"It's a city," I said. "In Kansas."

"Yeah, I know."

He walked over to the merry-go-round and made it spin. I dropped down to the sand underneath the monkey bars.

"Come on," he said. "Let's ride."

I shook my head. "Go ahead."

I didn't want to tell him that the last time I rode on a merry-go-round I threw up.

He ran beside the whirling, so-obviously-sadistic contraption of metal and wood. He ran beside it, pushing hard, then jumped on and leaned back so his head was upside-down. Going around and around. I kept waiting for something bad to happen to him. At least he should turn green from spinning around upside-down. Nothing happened. Then he stuck his toe into the dirt and stopped the revolving death trap.

"Come on," he said again. "I'll push it. You can just ride."

I shook my head again.

He held out his hand. "Come on. Trust me."

I started to shake my head, then I grabbed his hand and hopped on. My palms started to sweat, and I could smell the rusty metal scent of the iron pipes coming up from between my fingers where I clutched the merry-go-round in a death grip. The platform beneath me rocked as he ran.

"Get on, get on," I screamed, frightened that he would push it as fast as he could and then run away. Berkeley had done that at the church playground.

He jumped up beside me. "I'm not going to leave," he said "I'm Jonah."

Then I threw up on him.

How can you be free of a friend? You can divorce a husband. Break up with a boyfriend. Run away from home. But the only way to lose a friend is to drift apart. I don't even know if I can drift away from Jonah. How do you drift away from a friend you've known nearly as long as you've known yourself?

"Are we on for The Club tonight?" Jonah asks through his scarf. "Or do you just want to hang out and pout about something?"

He can tell I'm unhappy. I've been unhappy a lot lately. I can tell he's getting annoyed by my silent unhappiness. I'm not a silent person. When I'm unhappy, I fall to the floor and begin to pound my hands and feet in a major temper tantrum. I inherited my anger management skills from my mother. It was one of the reasons I spent so much time in the weedy vacant lot behind our house when I was a kid. Mom spent a lot of time on the floor kicking and screaming. Usually at Dad. Or Grandma. Or the grocery store, because they didn't happen to have Pecan Sandies this week.

So my genetic inheritance means I'm not usually silent in my unhappiness. Jonah knows this. I know that he knows this. And I know that my being unhappy and not loud about it is driving him crazy.

"The Club," I say, ignoring his invitation to talk in favor of his invitation to continue pretending nothing's wrong.

I can feel Jonz frown. "Okay."

The Club is not a club. You won't see it on some ridiculous TV show about life in the city. It's not the kind of club that knows your name, either. It's a dirty hole in downtown Chicago. With a constant open-mike night. Jonz and I discovered The Club when Kenny was going through his "I'm gonna be a rock star" phase. Kenny liked the open-ended opportunity of a consistent open mike. It wasn't long before Kenny was banned from The Club. Jonz and I kept going. Despite gossip to the contrary, there really aren't that many people with a voice like Kenny's—part yodel, part howl—and most of the time, The Club just plays Robert Johnson or Son House tunes over the stereo system. Mostly Jonz and I go there to avoid Kenny.

"We don't have to go," Jonz says, "if you'd rather do something else."

"The Club is fine," I say, continuing the charade.

He stops in the middle of the sidewalk. I walk a few steps before I give in and turn around to look at him. "What?" I ask.

He steps up and looks down into my face. His eyes are so brown they're almost black. I look like a ridiculous, swathed, twin Humpty-Dumpty in the brown-black depths. It was a never-ending source of frustration that Jonah kept growing after I stopped at five foot six or so. He kept growing to just a little over six feet. Now I have to look up at him. I used to stand on tiptoe so I could (sort of) meet him on eye level. Now looking up doesn't bother me. Correction. It *didn't* bother me. Right now it bugs me a lot.

"What's up with you?" he asks.

I shrug. The gesture loses its eloquence beneath a turtleneck, a sweater, and a heavy wool steamer coat. "Nothing."

A noise catches our attention. Two starlings fighting over a hot dog wrapper from the stubborn stand on the corner.

Jonz shakes his head and smiles under his scarf. "C'mon, Cheetah," he says, throwing an arm over my shoulder.

The heat from his arm and side worms its way through the wool, through the sweater, through the turtleneck, until it touches the center of my chest.

• • •

I was a junior in high school when Morgan moved to town. The girl with the cowboy name was from New York City, and she was too big, too blond, too hip for a "piece of shit town on the prairie," as she put it. All the boys instantly fell in love. Morgan was a cheerleader, and she could wave those red pom-poms and jiggle all at the same time. Male tongues fell limp onto the tables when Morgan's green Volvo whipped past the town's lone Burger King. Jonz and I didn't live in Chicago back then. We lived in Hove—an Illinois town that barely qualified to be in the Rand McNally Road Atlas. Morgan's New York City daddy had made his money and broken his brain on Wall Street. His wife brought him back to her girlhood home so she could feed him a liquid diet through a straw while Morgan fed the local boys on a heady diet of excitement and danger. The poor local boys. They'd never seen a real, live giraffe, much less an exotic animal like Morgan.

"It's disgusting," I said for the Nth time as Morgan's green Volvo sped past the Burger King's window and male heads twirled like yo-yos on a string. "It's disgusting how all the guys drool. Don't they have any dignity?"

"Mmm," Jonz said around a mouthful of fries.

It was Wednesday. Wednesday was Burger King day. (Just like Monday, Tuesday, Thursday, and Friday.) Jonah and I would sneak out and have lunch at Burger King. Jonah and I and all the other students at the high school.

"You don't think it's disgusting?" I asked.

"It's biology," Jonz said. "She's the new female in the herd, so all the males are interested. You can't blame them. Blame a few billion years of evolution."

I felt proud to be sitting with the only guy who could calmly talk about biology and Morgan—together—in such a clinical, doctor sort of breath.

Until I found Jonz rocking the green Volvo with Morgan on Saturday night.

Sitting across from Jonz in our booth at The Club, I lean back into the corner made by the cracked leather seat and the wall. On a good day, I probably wouldn't want to lean against the wall, but tonight isn't a good day. The Club isn't heated in any normal sense of the word, which accounts for people huddling in booths and not taking off their coats. After an hour or two, human body heat will turn the place into an oven. At that point, we'll all shed our skins like so many snakes.

Jonz leans into the table and wraps his fingers around a mug of The Club's best coffee. Coffee. It's one thing The Club does really well. Strong, black, and hot enough to pierce the thickest buzz at closing time.

"It's cold," he says.

"The coffee?" I ask, surprised.

"No. Outside." He looks up, tilts his head to one side. "Inside. Are you okay?"

Smoke swirls up to the stamped-tin ceiling. My fingers start to itch. The dedication I feel toward quitting can be measured by the fact that I have a pack in my coat pocket. It may have been left there since last week when I threw its brothers into the trash, but I've worn my coat every day since so it seems unlikely. I probably bought it in a lack-of-nicotine haze. I tap out a cigarette and light it from the candle—The Club's attempt at atmosphere—sitting on the table.

"I thought you quit," Jonz says.

"*Mañana*." I blow a cloud up to join the smoke curling around the ceiling.

He's looking at me. From the way the creases appear around his eyes, I know he's having the same memory I'm having.

• • •

I ran all the way home that night—the night I found Jonah and Morgan rocking the green Volvo. All I could see was Morgan's red pom-poms bouncing on the back dash. Bouncing, bouncing, bouncing with each slam my running shoes made on the cement sidewalk.

Mom was still up when I banged through the screen door and into the kitchen. She was dunking a Pecan Sandie into a cup of decaf. No caffeine after five P.M., no exceptions. I grabbed a Coke and started to head for my room, but her voice stopped me.

"Is that caffeine-free?"

I held up the can for her to see and tried not to let her see my face. Dirt and tears would cause questions, and I was pretty sure I had dirt on my face. Tears . . .

I don't remember.

"You need to stop hanging around with that boy," Mom said. "I'd have put a stop to it by now, but your father won't hear of it. Says it's harmless." She snorted. "Harmless. There's nothing harmless about it. Look at you. It's nearly midnight, and here you are."

I kept my mouth shut and my eyes on the stairs to the bedrooms. Normally, I would have started screeching around the "harmless" part of the lecture, but my brain was too overwhelmed by red pom-poms.

"You're a sight!" Mom continued. "Running around all over town. People will talk."

People talked, all right. They talked about Mom's trips to the grocery store and Dad's trips to the post office to see Dolores. They didn't talk about me. I never did anything half as exciting as Mom and Dad.

"Good night, Mom," I said before she could work up a good head of indignation.

"Someday you'll wish you'd listened to me," Mom said. "When you're knocked up and wondering where that boy is."

Up in my room, I popped the can of Coke open and stared at the window. Before the can was half finished, a rock hit the glass. I waited. More rocks. I still waited. Maybe I wanted to punish him a little, make him worry I wouldn't open the window.

It wasn't like he couldn't have just gone to the door and asked for me. For all her talk, Mom would have let him come in and hang out. As long as we stayed downstairs, where she could hover in the shadows. But we had seen the rocks-window thing in a Saturday afternoon movie when we were kids and had decided it would be our only means of communication from then on. Illicit communication. Like the secret handshake all the Masons are supposed to have.

I pushed the window open. "Hey."

"Hey." In the glow from the downstairs windows, I could see that his face was flushed. Whether it was from Morgan or from bending over hunting for rocks, I didn't know.

Looking up, he pushed the hair out of his eyes. And I decided to forgive him for being as stupid as the rest of the idiots at school.

Because that's why I felt all twisted up inside.

Nothing like finding out your best friend is an idiot.

I lifted a leg over the windowsill and reached out for the tree limb nearest me. When I had a good grip, I let my full weight hang from my hands. The limb bowed down until I hung only four feet from the ground. I let go and landed beside Jonah. His eyes were closed.

"I'm down," I said.

His eyes opened. He never could watch while I did that. I hate spinning around. Jonz hates heights.

I sniffed the air. "You smell like Morgan," I told him. "Were you doing a biology experiment?" Then I grinned, so he would know I was okay with that.

9

He looked at me and frowned, with that little way he has of frowning. I know it's there even when I can't see it. His eyes scrunch at the corners— like when he smiles, only different—and his forehead wrinkles. But you can only guess the part about his forehead because it's hidden under that black hair.

"It may have been an experiment," he said, "but she didn't know about it."

"She didn't notice, huh?" I said.

"Fuck you," he said, all adult and unconcerned and smelling like Morgan's sweat. Then he pulled out a pack of cigarettes.

"She gave you that?" I asked.

"No. Here." He tapped one out and gave it to me.

I took it. "Isn't this what you're supposed to be doing with her?"

"It's what I'm doing with you," Jonz said.

I blow a cloud of smoke up to join the swirls just under the tin ceiling. Jonz is looking at me. From the way the creases appear around his eyes, I know he's having the same memory I'm having.

Chapter 2

Before we can dip into maudlin memories, my cell phone rings. Jonz blinks, and I stub out the cigarette and grope around in my coat for the phone.

"I want out," someone female says, but she says it at the same time that Mike—The Club's owner-bartender—decides to pop in some Jimi Hendrix. Which means Mike and his current girlfriend just called it quits. When things are good, Mike plays the blues. When things are bad, it's "All Along the Watchtower."

"Hold on," I say into the phone. "Be back in a minute," I say to Jonz. "I think it's Geena."

Outside the bar, the wind cuts through the smoke and nicotine buzz. I lean back against the wall and stick my free hand into my armpit to keep warm. "Geena?" I ask. "I can hear you now."

"I want out," Geena says again. Then she starts to cry.

Geena is my younger sister. Much younger. She's the result of the last time Mom and Dad tried to have a "normal" marriage. Whatever normal means. I think it means pancakes, bacon, and smiles coated in syrup, all dished out over the breakfast table. At least that's what Mom and Dad thought normal meant. Then Mom got pregnant and collapsed in grocery aisle number three, screaming about their cookie selection. Her stomach got bigger and Dad's smiles over breakfast got thinner. I was twelve and didn't much care either way.

I didn't like pancakes.

Geena is sixteen now, which makes me . . . Good God. Twenty-eight.

I fumble for the pack before I remember I don't have a lighter or matches or any other form of combustible. "Out of where?" I ask Geena. Her tears have dried up enough for her to talk.

"Out of here." She sniffs. "I want to come live with you."

Okay. No need for nicotine. That sentence is rush enough. I love Geena—she *is* my little sister. And she's a doll. Red hair, freckles, and legs like Barbie. But I'm not prepared to play house with an unhappy teenager. So that sentence scares me to death.

"Live with me?" I ask.

"I swear I'll get a job and help pay rent and everything."

"Um . . ." How to explain that I'm not the only one living in my apartment? There's my roommate. India. India might not feel the familial love necessary to cope with Geena's makeup all over the sink and her hair in the shower drain. "I have a roommate," I say. "I'd have to ask her if you could stay with us for a while."

"I want to *live* there," Geena says.

"Look . . ." I give up. "What's going on?" I ask instead. But I don't really have to ask.

"I hate you."

Those were the last words out of my mouth before I slammed the door of the house in the "piece of shit town on the prairie." But I could still hear Mom screaming through the door as I ran down the porch stairs. A week before, I'd taken half the money I'd been saving from the pitiful Burger King salary and had bought a car. The car wasn't much better than the town. But it had only taken half my money. The other half would help fund living expenses for the first semester at the University of Chicago. By some miracle of benign munificence, I had received a letter saying I was a good little writer so why not toddle on over to Chicago and take my chances?

Mom was furious when I came downstairs with my suitcase. "You're actually leaving? You're leaving me with a five-year-old baby to take care of?"

"You had the baby. It's your baby."

"I got this baby trying to keep your father around so you could have a normal life."

"Try a condom next time," I had yelled back through all the sound and fury of the last days of being seventeen. I had wanted someone to be proud of me. Be happy with me. I should have known pride wasn't forthcoming when all Mom and Dad had said about the letter from Chicago was, "We'll see."

"And just what do you know about condoms?" Mom asked, her eyes narrowing.

"More than you do, obviously."

And I left, but not before throwing the parting shot about my feelings over my shoulder.

"I hate her," Geena says. "I hate him."

You'd think that after the baby-producing attempt at "normal," my dad would have gone to Dolores and left Mom with her cookies. He didn't. Maybe they need each other. Maybe they can't find anyone else who can absorb all the anger they have to give.

"For a while," I say. "I need to talk to India, but you can come for a while."

Geena snuffles into the phone. "I want to *live* with you," she says again.

I bite my tongue before I can say "we'll see."

We settle little details like directions and transportation before she hangs up. Geena's never bothered to get a job, so it's not surprising that she doesn't have a car. Someone named Dylan will drive her. I picture two teens screaming across the prairie at ninety and dying from too much freedom. Mom will like that. It'll give her something else to blame on me. *"Then, while she was driving to see you, she died in that fiery car crash."*

Yeah. All my fault.

I squeeze the bridge of my nose between my finger and thumb. I'm cold and confused and worried about Geena and what I'm going to say to India and how I'm going to drift . . . so I go back into The Club.

Jonz is sitting where I left him. I wish he'd throw an arm over me and let me feel the warmth in the center of my chest again.

Only that's why we have to drift apart.

He looks up at me and smiles. But the smile never hits the corners of his eyes.

We were sitting cross-legged on Jonah's bed. His mom refused to air-condition the upstairs of their house, and heat wave ripples slunk in through the open window and fluttered the curtains.

"Do it again," Jonah said.

I stretched out my tongue and touched my nose.

It was summer. After the euphoria of freedom wears off, summer turns into days spent hashing thirteen-year-old philosophy and the exploration of odd bodily capabilities. In my case, touching my nose with my tongue.

"That is so weird," Jonz said.

"It's not weird," I said. "You can spit by pulling your tongue back. That's weird."

"Anyone can do that."

"I can't." I opened my mouth, pressed the underside of my tongue to my upper teeth, and promptly spit on him.

"Guess you can," he said.

"Know-it-all."

"Your ears twitch when you laugh."

"Yeah? Well your eyes get all scrunchy." I reached out and touched the skin by his left eye. "Right *there*."

He jerked back from my hand.

I put my hand down into my lap.

"It's hot up here," I said.

"*Jo*-nah!" came his mother's voice from downstairs. The house shuddered as something fell over, and her muttered "*damn*" rolled up the stairs just behind the sound of glass hitting hardwood and spraying out in fifty directions.

"You'd better go," Jonz said as he got up off the bed. "It sounds like she's started early."

His voice gave me the shivers. Even at thirteen. Maybe because I *was* thirteen, and the world was starting to look a lot bigger than the globe in the school hallway.

"Will you be okay?" I asked.

He smiled. "No problem." Only the skin by his eyes didn't go all scrunchy.

I sit down and pretend I can't see that Jonah isn't smiling with his eyes. Reaching across the table, I steal his coffee and take a few hot gulps in between telling him what Geena said.

"Why does she want to come here?" Jonz asks.

I roll my eyes. "She lives with my mother."

One corner of his mouth twitches. "Okay. Not that I blame her for wanting to move here. I'm still asking."

"She says she hates Mom and Dad, and she and some guy named Dylan are driving up. India's going to kill me."

"Can I have your CDs?" he asks, all sympathy and concern.

"No. I'm donating them to the morgue, along with your body parts." I lay my forehead on the table. "I don't want to be a mom," I say.

"She's sixteen," Jonah says. "You left when you were seventeen. You didn't have anybody and you turned out okay. I doubt she needs a mom."

"*I had you,*" I start to say, then shut my mouth. "I'm getting tired of 'Watchtower,'" I say instead. "Did Mike lose again?"

Jonah leans back into his seat, silently acknowledging my need for a bit of space on the play-Geena's-mommy thing. "I got the coffee myself," he says. "Didn't talk to him."

"I want a beer," I say, sliding out. "You need some more coffee?"

He hands me his cup.

I've never bothered to ask Jonz why he's a teetotaler. The only liquid *I* ever saw his mother drink came out of the kitchen faucet. I guess I've always accepted that one hot summer afternoon interrupted by breaking glass and Jonah's vague "She's started early" as the explanation. But I've never actually asked. Looking down at the empty coffee cup, I wonder if it's a sign that Jonah and I aren't actually joined at the hip. My not asking, I mean.

Jonz is watching me with that careful consideration he gives to a painting by some long-dead nut with one eye. Or was that ear? Either way, it makes me nervous, so I shrug away the possible sign and smile at him before walking away.

"Hi, Mike," I yell to the shaggy man behind the bar. He pushes his hair back over his shoulder and nods to me to let me know he's heard my cry in the wilderness of Jimi's vocals. Mike reminds me of one of those medieval ascetics holed up in Holy Land caves. One of those medieval ascetics after a few decades without soap and a razor. Appearances aren't Mike's strength. Which probably explains the cracked leather seats and less-than-sanitary walls.

"'Watchtower' again, huh?" I say—yell—as I hand him Jonz' cup and point to the tap before holding up one finger.

Mike shakes his head as he pours a glass of beer for me. "Ran off with my best friend."

"Guess he wasn't your best friend," I say.

He looks at me as if the thought hadn't occurred to him until this very moment. "Guess you're right," he says, setting the beer on the counter. "Caf or decaf?"

"Caf."

He leans his big hands on the counter after setting the coffee mug down next to the beer. "Two-fifty. Including the cup your friend took when my back was turned." He says it with a smile. Coffee is free at The Club. Mike just likes to point that out in little ways. Free coffee is an old taproom tradition, but a lot of the new clubs—the ones with colored lights and too many televisions—don't care much about tradition. After all, Starbucks charges more for a cup of coffee than most places charge for two fingers of whiskey. So to hell with tradition, right? But Mike likes tradition. And he likes to remind you that he likes tradition.

"Thanks for the coffee," I say, smiling, as I pay for the beer.

He slips the dollars into the register. "Is it too loud? Do you want me to turn it down?" he asks, pointing over his shoulder to the CD player.

This is new. Mike always stops conversations after the free coffee–tradition bit. I blink a few times, then look up at the CD player and the green lights bouncing around up at the top of the little volume indicator. Jimi delves into a wail and gnashing of teeth on guitar strings.

"Um . . . sure. Sure."

"Maybe . . ." He ducks his head. "Maybe something different?"

I bend down to see his face. He's blushing. "Mike, you always play Jimi when the girl leaves."

"Yeah, but . . ."

I lean over the counter and pull a Blues Collection CD out of the stack. "Play this," I say, pointing to the first song.

"Billie Holiday?" he asks. Then he looks at the title and smiles.

I carry the beer and coffee back to the table as Billie starts singing about how she's "got it bad, and that ain't good."

Jonz stares at me. "Where's your magic wand?" he asks.

Scrunching into the booth again, I glance over at Mike in time to see him duck his head and blush. Then he attacks the bar with a rag and a fanaticism usually reserved for a trainee with Merry Maids.

"I think it might be one of those things that can be used for good or evil," I say to Jonah. "I may be wishing for Jimi Hendrix pretty soon."

"Just so you don't have to kiss him good night," he says.

"Jimi?"

Jonah laughs, but there's a twinge of something in his face that doesn't match the creases by his eyes.

Ch ap te r   3

I finally gave up on trying to get people to pronounce my name correctly. Or incorrectly, depending on how you want to look at it. After a semester or two of roll call, I realized that professors tended to rhyme Wichita with "ta-ta" rather than "saw." One of the pronunciational benefits of living in the city as opposed to the little town on the prairie. So I gave up on correcting people. It means that Jonz gets some odd looks when he calls me Cheetah, but I'm used to that.

"Need a piggyback home?" Jonah asks when we step out into the night cold.

It's an old joke. We made a bet once that he couldn't carry me for a city block. He did. I lost. But lately, I'm scared to touch him.

I need him too much.

I rely on him too much.

When I have a problem, I turn to Jonz. When I'm sad, I call Jonz and he comes over and pats my shoulder while I sigh and moan. When I'm angry . . . Well, Jonz doesn't laugh when I hurt my hand hitting things that are too hard to hit.

Blame my problem on India. She's the best roomie I've ever had. She does her dishes. It seems like a small thing, but the last roommate I had thought she was a gourmet cook and dirtied enough dishes to prove it. In addition to lots of pots, heavy skillets, knives, and cutting boards, gourmet cooks usually have dishwashers. My apartment has a sink fueled by the power of the human hand. India doesn't know gourmet from glutton—she eats a lot of packaged salads and Cap'n Crunch—but she knows how to run hot water and make it soapy. So I'm not complaining about India.

But one day, after Jonz blew in with me, gave me a big smack on the cheek, then blew out, India said, *"You guys are like married or something. Are you joined at the hip?"*

Whatever.

Then I saw the TV report about the Siamese twins joined at the head. They were from some place like Afghanistan or Kazakhstan or some kind of -stan, and they were coming to some place like Johns Hopkins. . . . Okay, I don't remember the details real well, but the important point is that here were these two babies and their skulls were grown together, and the doctors didn't know if there was enough brain to keep them both alive or if there was just one brain or two. And I sat and looked at the TV screen and thought, *"Omigod, do I have my own brain?"*

Or am I just a part of Jonah? Jonah's brain, I mean.

So it's all India's fault because she said that bit about Jonz and I being joined at the hip. And it was like when people have those epiphanies—I think that's what it's called when you suddenly realize something—and then keep on finding confirmation that the epiphany is correct. Like, for example, if a wife suddenly thinks, "My God! He's cheating on me!" and then she starts finding receipts for flowers she never saw and hotels just blocks from home. . . .

India says, "Are you joined at the hip?" and I laugh, but then I see the report on the Siamese twins and I start wondering if Jonz and I are joined at the brain.

Do I have my own thoughts? Can I move, say, this little finger on my own, or does Jonah have to think it first? Can I walk. . . .

But you get the point.

So when Jonz asks me if I want a piggyback ride home, I start to wonder if we're joined at the chest or the heart or the lungs.

And I'm scared to touch him because I'm afraid we'll fuse together and I'll never find out if I'm capable of breathing independently. This is a really sad place to be when you're twenty-eight years old and you've been away from home for eleven years and you've got an MFA in creative writing and you're killing yourself writing up grant proposals for a down-in-the-hoof neighborhood museum and you have relationships but they never work out because the male brain is so *dense.*

And in the middle of this, I get to play wise woman to my little sister and some guy named Dylan. Well, maybe not wise woman, but hostess-cum-therapist, anyway. Or—hellish thought—Mommy dearest.

"Hey!" Jonz says, waving a hand in front of my face.

"Put your gloves on," I tell him, practicing for my mommy role.

He pinches my nose and ruins my parental dignity. "Give up now," he says, digging in his pockets for his gloves. "You're not mommy material."

"Yeah, I know." Being a mommy is one of those things I vowed to never do. I'm no good at putting flowers in my own hair, much less . . . Okay, that's going to require some explanation.

I went out with Filthy Jeff Scaletti once. Because he would sit on the carpet-covered stage at the front of the cafeteria every morning just so he could say, "Hi, Wichita." Because he was a lonely outsider and I felt sorry for him. Because after I said I'd go out with him, someone left a clothespin on my locker door.

Jeff didn't bathe. He did PE like everyone else, but he didn't take a shower after he got all sweaty. His jockstrap was a school joke. He had earwax so thick you could see it if you weren't careful to avoid looking at him from the side.

Filthy Jeff.

I felt sorry for him. No one should be treated like a piece of shit. Ever. And being treated like a piece of shit before you have the opportunity to act like one . . . Life dumps enough unpleasant stuff on a person. Why do some jerks always feel compelled to add a little more?

I said I'd go to the sophomore dance with him. I was in eighth grade, so it wasn't like it was cool for him to ask me or anything. Maybe he just thought I wouldn't say no. Maybe I was the only person who said "hi" back every morning.

Mom loved the idea of her little girl going on a date. Baby Geena screamed in the background while Mom tried to weave flowers into my hair. It didn't work. My hair was brown silk. That's not a compliment. That's a nice way to say my hair was—is—so fine nothing sticks to it. The flowers kept sagging and dropping onto the bed.

"Hold still," Mom ordered when Geena paused to draw a breath and she was sure I could hear.

"Flowers are so dumb," I said, wiggling away.

Mom grabbed my hair and tugged me back. "You'll look nice for that boy if it kills me."

My scalp stung. "They won't stay," I said. "Just forget it."

Geena started screaming again.

Mom threw up her hands. "Fine. Go on. Let the big girls make fun of you, if that's what you want."

I slunk out of the bedroom.

The "big girls" made fun of me. But it wasn't because I didn't have flowers in my hair.

Jeff took a bath.

I'm not sure why taking a bath would be a reason for unbridled hilarity, but apparently cleanliness is next to humor as well as God.

"Hey, Jeff," one girl said, "you clean up nice." Then she and her friends did the pretty-girl snigger so common among the popular set.

Jeff just looked at her. All puzzled. Like a coonhound who doesn't get why the hunter wants him to kill that cute, furry raccoon.

"C'mon, Jeff," I said, grabbing his elbow and pulling him toward the food table. He started to dip up some punch, but I stopped him.

"It's spiked," I said, jerking my chin toward the side door of the gym, where Clyve, the janitor, was taking a swig from a small bottle. "Clyve spikes it every dance."

Jeff leaned over and sniffed the punch. "Smells fine," he said.

I didn't bother to tell him that no one could smell a darn thing over the cologne he was wearing.

"Trust me," I said.

And that made me think of Jonah. And the way Jonah had bent over laughing when I'd told him I was going to the sophomore dance with Filthy Jeff. Sometimes I wanted to punch Jonah in the nose. He could be such a jerk. Just that morning, Mom had kicked us both off the front porch because he kept telling me I had to kiss Filthy Jeff after the dance and I was loud in the assurances that kissing would not be on the evening's agenda. *"You two are a pair of goddamn starlings,"* Mom had yelled after us as we sulked off to school. *"Always pecking at each other."*

And that was how Mom found out I had a date with Filthy Jeff and I ended up sitting on her bed with flowers dropping around me like rain.

Jonah still owes me for a sore scalp and the stupid flowers hanging in my eyes. And I just can't see myself fussing with flowers and boys and scream-ing babies. It looks like I'll get to skip the babies part and move right on into the teen years. Depending on whether Geena is more grown up than she was the last time I saw her.

Which was . . . four or five years ago.

I don't get home a lot.

"Still thinking about the piggyback offer?" Jonz asks.

I try to smile and not picture soul-body fusion. "No," I say, struggling to find a decent excuse. "I . . . I think I'd better get back home before India goes to bed so I can talk to her about Geena."

He has that look of potential protest on his face—the one that says he knows something is going on that's bugging me and he's frustrated because I'm not using an exterminator—but then he shrugs. "Fine."

"I'll just take a taxi," I say, knowing it isn't in my budget.

"Fine." Just "fine." He doesn't offer to split it or ask for a ride or argue about my budget.

"See you, then," I say, flagging down a taxi. I don't offer to split it or give him a ride or defend my extravagance.

He nods. "See you tomorrow." Then he turns and walks away.

I climb into the taxi, give my address, then sit back to think.

I'm behaving badly. I'm treating Jonah like he's a piece of shit and he's never done . . . well, maybe that time . . . No. He's never done anything to deserve being treated like a piece of shit. But I'm doing it anyway because I'm incompetent.

I'm not an incompetent person. When I start out to do something I've never done before, I do a lot of research. I go to the library, check out every book on the subject that's ever been written, and read them all. Or at least skim them all, depending on how thoroughly hashed the subject is. Then, armed to the teeth with expert opinions, I step out into the world and do battle.

I went to the library after my Siamese twin epiphany. The library is a great place for books by experts. The fiction shelf has shrunk in recent years because everyone demands the popular-expert book of the hour. The fiction shelf loses ground every week to books on losing ten pounds in thirty days, books on keeping your man, books on leaving your man, books with twelve-step programs for success, books with eight-step programs to instant popularity, books on how to kill armpit mushrooms by eating only hamburger and yogurt for six weeks. . . . And the literature of the world languishes on a shelf in the dim part at the back.

But none of those experts had expert advice on how to leave a friend. Lots of advice about attracting friends, but not one with advice on how to be a friend repellent. Or how to separate Siamese twins, for that matter.

So I'm pretty much on my own here. And I'm incompetent.

". . . here?" the taxi driver asks.

"What?"

"Isn't that," he jerks his thumb toward the passenger-side window, "the address?"

I look up and see my apartment building. "Oh. Yeah. Thanks. I was thinking—"

"Yeah? Well, it's twenty-five."

"Bullshit. Ten. What's the meter say?"

He smiles a big eight-step program smile. "Meter's broken."

A stupid, newbie mistake. Not checking the meter when I got in. But I was preoccupied. I throw a ten onto the seat beside him and crawl out. The door to the building is six feet away, I know the fare is only ten, and I never did think much of the eight-step program.

"Fuck you!" the taxi driver says as he pulls away. But it's one of those "Sorry I didn't get you that time" kind of insults. The kind with no heat. One of the perks of living in Chicago—union land—instead of Hove. When you all work for a living, it's hard to get too distraught over a little arm wrestling with each other, since everyone's used to having their arms twisted by the people who get rich for doing nothing but owning stock in a company.

India is watching some "Where did those old rock stars go?" program when I open the door.

"I have bad news," I say.

"Your sister called," she says at the same time. "She's lost somewhere out by Joliet and she couldn't reach your cell."

"That's the bad news," I say after absorbing this blow. Geena obviously didn't tell me how far out of Chicago she was when she called.

"What? Your cell batteries are dead?" India asks, turning off the TV just in time to rescue us from some '80s stadium rock.

"Geena wants to live with us."

India looks down at the remote.

"I told her she could stay for a while, but I didn't say anything about living here."

India keeps looking at the remote.

"She's had a fight with Mom and Dad," I say, starting to get that desperate feeling in my stomach. "Some guy named Dylan is with her."

"Yeah? He's the one who got them lost. At least that's what it sounded like." She looks up at me. "This is a two-bedroom apartment."

"I know."

"Not a three- or a four-bedroom."

"I *know.*"

She shakes her head. "You could have asked."

"I was going to," I say, realizing that I should have called her right away, but I was too caught up in my own mommy-dearest, friend-repellant thoughts. "I should have called you."

"Yeah."

"You do your dishes," I say. "I don't want to find a new roommate."

India laughs. "I'm not moving out," she says. "But I wouldn't want you to have to leave."

"Ha, ha. I don't want her here either, but—"

"She's your sister," India says, reproach thick in her voice. "You can't just give her a box and show her the alley."

I feel red heat crawl up my neck. "No, but—"

"So give her a week to find a job—"

"She's never had a job. I'm not sure she knows how to do anything but paint her nails."

India shrugs, reminding me of Jonz. "So give her a week, and then she and Dylan will be off finding their own place or slinking home like runaway puppies."

"You think?"

"No. But I can indulge in fantasies." She stretches, all feline grace and bones. The kind of sleek, thin woman who can wear leather and fur as if she grew it herself. I look a little like a corn-fed farm girl. It's not fair, actually. If I look corn-fed, at least I should look good in leather. After all, cows eat corn. Or does leather only come from steers? But steers eat corn, don't they? And which ones get the growth hormones? I can never remember the details.

"I'm sorry," I say to India, giving up on the cows. "I'll try and get rid of them as soon as I can."

She waves a hand. "Forget about it. But you might want to get them out of Joliet." She shudders. "All those suburbs . . . Ish."

I call the number Geena left. It's a Denny's somewhere. I describe my sister before I realize that she isn't twelve anymore. "Now try and imagine one of those aging things," I say, "like on the milk cartons."

The person on the other line is silent for a moment or two, then Geena says, "Wichita?"

The shock of hearing my name pronounced correctly is strong enough that I almost tell her she has the wrong number. "It's me," I say instead.

"We're lost somewhere near Joliet," she says.

"Did you ask anyone there for directions?"

Silence.

"Um . . . I guess we were hungry and we . . ."

I pinch the bridge of my nose and wish my sister had the homing smarts of a lost puppy. Which isn't a lot, but it's more than this.

"I'm sorry," Geena says. She covers the phone and asks someone—presumably the person with the mental artificial aging software—if they know how to get to Chicago.

I pinch my nose harder.

"We'll be there," Geena says. "An hour or so?"

Unless they get lost again and stop for doughnuts.

"Okay," I say. "Do you have the directions I gave you?"

"Yes." Then she hangs up.

"All peachy?" India asks.

"Just."

"Well, I'm going to take a bath. I don't think there'll be a lot of hot water in the future."

Chapter 4

Once upon a time in some long-forgotten college requirement course, I had a professor tell me that we were nothing more and nothing less than our genes. All our reactions, all our decisions, were somehow programmed into us by the mixed DNA of our ancestors. He then went on to use this argument to debate some Jungian collective-unconscious stuff, and the entire class went to sleep. And while sleeping, I dreamed I had developed a fondness for Pecan Sandies and emotional abuse. The thought was so horrifying, I forced myself awake. I opened my eyes and found I was the center of attention. An entire lecture hall's worth of eyes looking at me. I got a gold star for emitting not one but two primal screams.

We are not a collection of DNA. Well, okay, we are. But not like the prof meant it. We are a collection of memories. Our memories determine who we are, what we think, our reactions to stress, fear, pain, joy, love, sex. . . .

Memories. It's all in the memories.

Each one of us is nothing more than a box filled with memories.

India is making good on her promise to use all the hot water. I'm lying on the couch, listening to the water run and pretending to watch a sitcom while Geena's lost-puppy appearance in Joliet worries my conscious mind. Then the token senior citizen on the TV screen says, "My memory just ain't what it used to be"—or words that mean the same thing—and I find myself wondering what happened to a cigar box of memories.

The cigar box came into Jonah's and my possession in a roundabout kind of way. Sometime around the end of the second grade. We were walking home from school when we heard something sobbing in an alley. We almost missed it. It had been a bad day of pop quizzes on the multiplication tables and shepherd's pie in the cafeteria—which doesn't sound so bad until you think about industrial-strength mashed potatoes, mushy beans, and *E. coli*–laced hamburger. Not that we thought much about E. coli . . . But I'm drifting.

We almost missed the crying. I heard it first.

"There's someone in the alley," I said.

Jonz was already climbing over the boxes and trash.

I followed him, but I had to get my oversized backpack off first, so by the time I got over the boxes and stuff, he already had the puppy in his lap. He was crying. The puppy was crying. When I saw the puppy, I started crying.

The puppy was a mangled mess. He'd played with a car and lost, and no one had bothered to care.

"We need to take him to the vet," I said, touching the brown, furry forehead.

Jonah swiped a hand under his nose. "Do you know where one is?"

I thought about it. "Yes."

We carried the puppy nearly a mile. I dumped all my books out of my backpack and left them under a box in the alley so we had something to carry the puppy in.

The vet in our town was a grizzled farm veteran who wore overalls and accessorized by clenching a cigar between his brown teeth. He had never intended to work on small animals. His training involved cattle, sheep, horses, pigs . . . farm animals. But if you're the only vet in a small town . . . well, towns have town people and town people have cats and dogs, not sheep and horses. So the vet was used to dealing with all kinds of livestock.

He also knew a hopeless case when he saw one.

Hours later, dirt under my fingernails, I shuffled home. I got a spanking for forgetting to get my books and for making Dad drive all the way back to the alley at nine o'clock at night.

I also got spanked for not showing up for supper. It took a long time for Jonah and me to bury the puppy.

I wasn't hungry anyway.

My cell phone rings and interrupts my brain midmemory. I'm not sure why I'm thinking about the puppy right now. Oh yeah. The cigar box. Memories. Lost-puppy sisters. My legs hurt from lying crunched up on the couch.

March fog mists the streetlights and the window over the kitchen table. India drifted off to bed hours ago, all warm and smelling of some exotic after-bath powder. I smell like Safeguard, and I'm still cold because I didn't wait long enough for the hot water heater to do its job.

The cell keeps ringing until I finally locate it in the pocket of my coat.

"Hello?"

"Wichita?"

Ah. The wayward sister and her darling. Who else?

"We're . . ." She pauses, then asks someone—the last of the surviving Lost Boys, presumably—"Where are we?"

A mumble.

Somehow they've drifted north. I try giving directions again, but it's not like I know the city inside and out. I go where I want to go, but I let Chicago Transit Authority do the driving. After three or four confused minutes, the lovebirds find a gas station.

More mumbling.

I yawn.

"Twenty minutes," Geena says into my ear.

I look at the clock. "It's two in the morning," I say. "Could you manage to not get lost again?"

But she's already hung up.

I drop back down onto the couch. Stare at the moving figures on the TV screen. Then some guy comes on to advertise a memory improvement program he's invented.

I hit the remote and the screen goes dark.

Lost puppies and cigar boxes.

Three days after we buried the puppy, Jonah and I were visiting the little mound. I had brought some purloined petunias from Mom's window boxes. Jonah had brought a dog biscuit. We had buried the puppy in one of the weedy lots that seem to populate the town of Hove as much as or more than people. The vet must have driven by and seen us.

"I have some work for you two," he said, after rolling down the dusty window of his truck. "Hop in."

In the office-slash-impromptu waiting room, we found a box filled with seven wiggly, rotund black puppies.

"Somebody just dropped them off," the vet said to us as we knelt beside the box. The puppies licked and squirmed and pawed at our fingers and smelled like that subtle puppy combination of warm milk and dog doo. "And they're bored, poor little things," the vet continued. "Until I can find homes for them . . . ?"

He ended on a question, but we both bowed our heads, knowing we'd

never be allowed to keep a puppy. Jonah had a dog. And me? I knew better than to ask.

The vet coughed. "Well, until I can find homes for them, they'll need
lots of love and attention. Thought maybe you two could help me."

And for the next three days, Jonah and I forgot, by burying our fingers in sleek puppy fur, the mangled brown body we had buried. On the
third day, the last puppy left us, tongue hanging over some other child's
shoulder. We stared after it and felt like crying.

"You did a good job," the vet said. "Seems like I ought to pay you
something." Willfully oblivious to the fact that he had already given us
more than we'd ever received in our lives. "I wonder what I could . . ." he
mumbled to himself as he reached out for a fresh cigar to replace the damp
stump in his mouth.

Jonz nudged me and pointed to the cigar box on the vet's desk. "Look
at that," he whispered.

We both leaned forward and admired the lady on the cardboard lid. A
full-blown, black-haired beauty in silk and velvet. Jonz never could resist a
painting. He reached out a finger and ran it around the figure. His skin
made a brushing sound on the cardboard.

"You two like that box?" the vet asked. Then he dumped out the
remaining cigars and handed it to Jonz. Too surprised to thank him, we
ran out the door.

Down the street, we stopped to admire the woman again, to open the
box and smell the tobacco smell.

"It smells like a memory," I said.

"Here," Jonah said. "Here's another memory." And he picked some
black hairs off of his shirt and dropped them into the cardboard confines.
"You too," he said. After a moment or two of tugging at my clothes, I
found a stiff puppy whisker. I laid it in the bottom of the box as reverently
as the priest down at St. Mary's laid out the host.

If I were to dig in that cigar box of memories, I wonder if I'd find those black hairs and that whisker, or if—after all the years of things put inside the cardboard walls—the hairs are lost in the memory tangle. I don't know. And I don't have the cigar box to find out, because after a month or two, the box stayed with Jonah. I'm not sure how or why. It just happened. Maybe because I keep my memories in my head. Where they can be sure to make me—keep me—who I am.

Three hours later, someone knocks on the door. I wake up in a cold knot on the couch and unwind enough to stumble over to the door and open it. Geena collapses dramatically into my arms as soon as I've worked the dead bolt and chain free. I catch her, hold her lost-puppy body next to mine.

"I'm pregnant," she says.

Chapter 5

I was nine when Mom sat me down on her bed and told me about boys and their "little sticks" they wanted to stick into me. I'd known about sex for . . . I don't know. At least two or three years. The conversation with my mom was painful and embarrassing. I squirmed on the pink comforter and tried to think about something else, but Mom grabbed my shoulders and shook me.

"Are you listening?" she said. "Listen to me, because I don't want a baby having a baby in my house. And with you running all over town with that little friend of yours . . ."

And from then on, the conversation degenerated into a scene that mimicked Jimi's guitar playing: lots of wailing and gnashing of teeth. Why couldn't I be like the other little girls, who were always good and sweet and played with Barbies? Why did I run around like a soon-to-be slut with that boy? Didn't I know that boys only wanted one thing from a girl? Girls and boys could never be friends. He'd do his stick trick, and I'd be left all alone.

This part didn't make me squirm. This was the part where I rolled my eyes behind Mom's back—being careful she couldn't see me in the giant rectangle of mirror over her dresser (I'd learned to watch out for that the hard way)—and waited for her to drain her brain of all the usual cliches.

Once we got back to "Why can't you play with Barbie?" I knew we'd made it full circle and freedom was just over the horizon.

Freedom meant running a few blocks until I ran into Jonah.

"What took you so long?" he asked the day I was nine and had my first lecture on sex proper.

I put my hands on my hips and glared at him, doing my best Mom imitation. "I hear you have a stick that does tricks."

Jonz stared at me, his mouth hanging open a little. "Huh?"

I pointed dramatically to a vague spot between his legs.

He blushed. "That's gross."

"Yeah? It's grosser the way Mom says it."

The blush faded. "Oh. Your mom talked to you about sex."

We sat down on the sidewalk's edge. I picked up a stick and poked at a leaf until I realized what I was doing and threw it away. "She says she wishes I played with Barbies," I said, as I dusted my hand on my shorts.

Jonz digested this. "I guess she doesn't know Joleen," he said.

I laughed. And secretly wished Mom *could* see what Joleen made Ken and Barbie do when she played house.

I wake up cold and stiff. Once I'd absorbed Geena's annunciation and realized I only had about ninety minutes left before my alarm took off, it seemed ridiculous to try and make up a bed on the floor for the two young lovers. I didn't expect to do much more than maintain my fetal position on the couch and wonder how I get into messes I don't make. But at some point—probably after my legs went numb from being pulled to my chest—I must have dropped off, because I faintly recall a dream about boys with sticks chasing me around the playground.

I wake up cold and stiff and dying for coffee. I can hear the familiar sound of India splashing water into the coffeemaker, and I silently bless her and her ancestors.

"Hey," she says when I stagger into the kitchen and sit down at the table.

"Hey." I cradle my head in my hands. At least my hands are cold and soothe the hot ache behind my eyes. "She's pregnant," I mumble from behind my palms.

Silence.

I peek out through my fingers.

India is in the middle of scooping coffee into the filter. She's staring at the measuring scoop. "Am I on one or three?" she asks after a moment of intense concentration.

"I wasn't watching."

"I'll just guess." She tosses in a few more scoops and turns on the pot.

"I don't know what I'm going to do," I say, watching her put away the coffee and pull out the box of Cap'n Crunch.

"Do you want a bowl?" she asks.

"Yeah. I could use a sugar rush."

"Why do you have to do anything?" she asks as she plunks the milk onto the table and hands me a bowl and spoon. "She's the one who's pregnant. How does that affect you? Beyond the housing situation, I mean."

I pour the Cap'n's finest into my bowl. How *does* it affect me?

"I guess because I know Mom will be useless," I say. "Geena needs someone. She came to me. It affects me."

India nods. "Okay. But what about the guy with her?"

I look up from the milk. "Have you seen him?"

"Bumped into him outside the bathroom. Is he the dad?"

"Got me. I didn't ask. If he is, he's not dad material."

India laughs. "Look at you. The girl moves out of the country, but she can't move the old-fashioned country ideals out of the girl." Impervious to my glare, she munches a spoonful of Cap'n Crunch. "So he's got a few tattoos and some nipple rings. That doesn't mean he isn't qualified to be a dad."

She's right.

I woke up thinking about my mother, and now I sound like her.

I drop my head onto the table, ignoring the slosh of milk from my overflowing cereal bowl.

"I'm becoming my mother," I say to no one in particular.

India laughs again. "Hell, no. From what you've told me, she's no good for laughs. You," she pokes the top of my head with her spoon, "you're good for laughs."

"Thanks."

"Anytime." She slides her chair back. "I gotta go or I'll be late."

"India," I say, stopping her before she leaves the kitchen.

"Yeah?"

"Thanks. For letting them stay here. I know it's a hassle and—"

"You're welcome," she interrupts. She starts to leave, then leans back into the room. "As long as they find their own place in the next few days."

I dump the rest of my cereal down the disposal, then sneak into my bedroom for some clothes. The room is dark. I tend to leave the curtains open so I can wake up with at least some gray glow on the walls, but Geena and Dylan have the place sealed up tight. The room is dark *and* it smells like unwashed teenaged bodies and cigarette smoke. The smoke smell annoys me. When I smoke, I open a window and lean out into the frozen air because I don't like parading the odor of stale cigarette around with me. On the way to the closet, I trip over a pair of boots, land on a pile of clothes, and fall over a bag.

Forget hospitality.

I open the curtains.

Geena rolls over. "Turn out the light," she says before pulling the blanket over her head. "We're trying to sleep."

She doesn't know it, but if I hadn't seen the way Dylan pulled her complaining, wretched self close to him in his sleep, I would have given her a box and showed her the alley.

Family be damned.

"And this is your little sister," Mom said to me from the hospital bed in Hove General's maternity ward.

Dad gripped my shoulder and leaned down to my ear. "It's not a monkey in a pink blanket, even though she looks like one."

Neither Mom nor I thought it was funny.

I wanted to be down under the bridge with the rest of my class. Picking up trash on a Saturday morning sounded great compared to shifting from foot to foot in this room.

"Go on," Mom said, ignoring Dad's comment. "Say hello to baby Geena."

"That's a dumb name," I said. At thirteen I knew everything about names. "Everyone will think you named her after the actress."

"Her name is Geena," Mom said through stretched lips. "And she's your family."

Family be damned.

I get off the bus a block early and hope the March wind will clean the smoke smell out of my hair and clothes. It's a stupid move. I'm freezing by the time I reach the museum. The wind follows me through the glass door, sending scraps of paper and last autumn's leaves skipping across the all-weather rug and down the tiled hall. But once the door closes, the museum wraps me up in the familiar smell of floor wax and crumbling hand-embroidered linens. Petroleum products scented with starch, age, and memories.

It's just a small museum. One of the myriad local-historical-society outfits that inhabit classic buildings and vie for tax dollars and grants while trying to keep Chicago's past from being locked up in a drawer. As the grant writer, it's my job to scrounge up enough money to keep history out in the open. Grant writer. It sounds more official than it feels in practice.

I stop by my office to offload my scarf, coat, and bag, and pick up my coffee cup. The cup is still rimmed with dried coffee from yesterday. I debate going to the restroom to wash it, then shrug and move on down the hall toward the siren sounds coming from the coffee room.

I don't mean sirens in the Ulysses-*Odyssey* kind of way. More in the air raid kind of way.

Kenny is in fine form this morning. (Kenny's the guy who helped create The Club's "everybody's welcome—except Kenny" open-mike policy.) When I say Kenny is in fine form, I mean he's demonstrating his latest vocal techniques. And I follow the sound down the dim hall and find half the museum's staff gathered around Kenny like rats around the Pied Piper. Only Kenny is using his voice to make that whistling sound. Dorothy appears to be undergoing a painful round of acupuncture. Timothy—he's the museum director and technically our boss, but you wouldn't know it by looking at him—Timothy's jaw is aligned with the top button of his flannel shirt.

And Jonz. Jonz is pretending to pour a cup of coffee, but he's laughing.

Ever since Jonz' front teeth came in, I've found his smile . . . enchanting. "Enchanting" is a really stupid word, but I can't come up with anything better. It's not because he has white teeth or even *straight* teeth. He doesn't have dimples. But when he smiles—really smiles, so the skin by his eyes scrunches up—the sun is warm, spring is here, and God just might exist.

Jonz hefts his coffee cup and turns.

Sees me.

Kenny's siren call fades into the distance. Outside the March fog still holds the city in its cotton grip, but inside . . . the sun shines just for me in the depths of Jonah's slow smile.

Why, in God's name, do I care if we're joined at the hip or the head or the heart?

The nauseating scent of pecans joins the honest coffee smell, and my stomach lurches, breaking the spell of Jonah's smile. Kenny hits a high E, and the microwave pops open, disgorging a piece of pecan-laced coffee cake. Dorothy grabs the cake and her mug.

"Here," she says, shoving the full mug into my free hand. "You can have my coffee if you'll help pull me away from his aura."

I'm still looking at Jonz, and it takes me a few heartbeats to realize she means Kenny. "He's sucking you in, huh?" I ask, shaking off the sudden chill as I break eye contact with Jonz.

She nods, grabbing my arm and tugging me toward the coffee room door. "I thought maybe someone was killing a cat, so I came in to check it out."

As we leave, Kenny switches to an Elvis tune. Not one of the lively, thin-Elvis songs. One of the Las Vegas ones. Dorothy and I make a show of pulling ourselves out of the room.

"Look," Kenny says in midsong, "women have to drag themselves away from me. I'm a chick magnet."

Timothy's jaw is still attached to his shirt. "How do you *do* that?" he asks as Dorothy and I make our escape.

"If you can't sing," I hear Kenny say to Timothy, "you can always try a different brand of cologne. Bees to honey."

"I'm never sure if he's being serious or if he's just got a really great sense of humor," Dorothy says, releasing my arm now that we're free of Kenny's magnetic personality.

"You thought that was funny?" I ask, wishing I had a free hand to rub the spot where her fingers have squeezed the blood from my arm.

"No."

"I guess that answers your question then."

"Maybe." She shakes her head and walks on past my office door, leaving me holding the two coffee cups.

The nauseating scent of pecans swirls in her wake.

The cookie bag rustled as Mom sat down in the chair next to mine. Just past the dusty glass of the living room windows, the Saturday morning sun turned the pavement white-hot. Cartoons flickered in front of me.

"Honey, you can always talk to me. I'm here for you," Mom said, her breath smelling like pecans and butter.

Then she started crying. "You never talk to me. You just sit there. He just sits there. Why doesn't anyone talk to me?"

Talk.

It's a dirty word. A dirty word that means too many things for it to even be classified as a simple word.

"Because you don't want to listen."

I didn't say it. Dad did. He was pulling on a T-shirt and getting ready for a Saturday morning walk to the post office. I'm not sure if Mom ever figured out the post office wasn't open on Saturdays.

"I listen," Mom said.

I kept my eyes on the cartoons, but I wasn't seeing anything. I wanted to be out frying on the sidewalk, out back in the weedy lot, dead and buried underground . . . anything to not be still sitting in the chair pretending to watch cartoons.

"You've never listened in your life." Dad bent over to look under my chair for his shoes.

Mom pulled herself up straight and tugged her housecoat tighter across her body. "You never *talk* to me. You tell me about the faucet in the kitchen. You tell me to call a plumber. You tell me I can have the car tomorrow. You tell me you'll be gone next week. You tell me . . . lots of things. But you never talk."

Dad pulled out his shoes. Brown-and-white shoes. As if a pair of golf shoes had mated with a pair of wingtips and produced offspring.

"Talk, talk, talk," Dad said. "You want to do all the talking, but you can't hear a word I'm saying."

I slipped out of my chair and made a run for the door.

"You get back here, young lady," Mom yelled after me. "I want to talk to you."

But I didn't get back there . . . or anywhere. I ran out the door, scaring a group of starlings that had been drinking the last of the water in the birdbath. The birds looked down at me from the electrical line.

Suddenly, I hated them. Hated the fact that they couldn't do anything without each other.

"Talk, talk, talk," I screamed, flapping my arms.

The starlings spread their wings and left the wires in a graceful arc.

I didn't go back into the house for hours.

Mom and I never talked.

I don't know how long I've been standing in the hallway. Not long enough for the coffee in Dorothy's cup to get cold, but long enough for the smell of pecans to drift away.

"Cheetah," Jonz says from behind me. I don't even jump. I knew he was there. Not on a conscious level. More on the level experienced by the bits and pieces from the Big Bang as they spin away from each other. Farther and farther into the black void, but always aware of the stars and planets and asteroids and dust beside them, above them, below. . . .

I knew Jonah was there.

"Can I talk to you?" he asks.

"Sure." I hand him the empty coffee cup so I can turn the doorknob.

I like my office. I once told India that I took this job because I got an office with a door, an oak desk, and a window. Actually, I took the job because my student loans were due, because Jonz put in a good word for me with Timothy, and because grant writing is still writing. Creative writing, even, depending on how closely the museum fits the grant requirements.

I like my office, but my hands are shaking. The pecan smell . . . it must have slid under my door. And it resurrects the images of my mother clinging, grasping, pecking at Dad. . . .

"You two are a pair of goddamn starlings. Always pecking at each other."

And I remember why a sunshine smile isn't enough. Why wishing on a shooting star—

I don't want to go there.

"So, what do you want to talk about?" I ask Jonz after I slip behind the safety of my desk. "Have a seat."

I'm proud of the casual way it comes out.

Silence.

I look up.

He's staring at the chair in front of my desk, his dark hair hanging down so I can't see his face. Only I know. . . .

"Jonah," I whisper. *Ah, Jesus. I don't want to hurt you, but I can't—*

He catches the thought before I finish it. "Later," he says. And he turns to leave.

"Jonz!" It's more of a cry for help this time.

He stops, but he doesn't turn around. And I don't know what I was going to say, so I wait for him to turn around so I don't have to say anything at all.

● ● ●

"Mom says no one ever talks to her," I told Jonah. It was the afternoon of the Saturday I had made my escape and we were sitting on the swings in the middle of the park and eating pistachio nuts. We would reach into the bag, pick a large nut, pull the shells apart to get at the green meat, then see how loud and obnoxious we could be about chewing. Jonz always won, but I did my best to chew like Mom had taught me not to. That is, mouth hanging open, food showing, lips smacking. A string or two of saliva helped, but I never could get decent viscosity.

"You talk to her," Jonz said, tossing empty shells.

"No, I don't. She talks all the time. She talks *at* me."

"That's what parents do." He puffed out his chest a little, as if what he had said was profound. Then he let the air out. His chest collapsed, and he reached for the bag of nuts. "Except on TV. But that's just crap."

I dug a toe into the sand. Jonah twisted the chains of his swing together until he could pick up his feet and spin around. I closed my eyes to keep from losing all the pistachios in my stomach.

"Sorry," Jonz said when the swing stopped.

"No problem. How come we can talk?"

He looked at me. "Because we don't need to."

I frowned.

"No, it's true." He closed his eyes. "What am I thinking about right now?"

"You want another pistachio, and then you want to do that thing with your swing until I puke on you."

He opened his eyes. "See? We don't have to talk. We *know* each other."

I wait for Jonz to turn around so I don't have to say anything at all. For one awful moment, I'm a spinning planet about to crash into its neighbor and explode into a million billion dust particles. . . . then he turns and looks at me.

And smiles.

"Here." He reaches into the inner pocket of his jacket and tosses me a vending machine bag of pistachios.

I catch them in midair. For one careless moment, nothing has changed.

Chapter 6

It's Eugene Scheiffelin's fault. A fan of Shakespeare, the New York drug manufacturer wanted to see all the birds of the bard flying the skies of the New World. Most of the time, it didn't work. The thrushes died. The skylarks died. Then around 1890 or so, Scheiffelin imported the starling.

The starling isn't a prominent character in Shakespeare. One line. One of the Henry plays. *Henry IV*, I think. But one line from Shakespeare caused the importation of one hundred birds into New York. The speckled immigrants settled down in the gutters of the American Museum of Natural History. Everyone thought it was cute until they pooped all over it.

Fifty years later, starlings covered the landscape from Alaska to Florida. Pecking, squeaking, pooping, fighting, proliferating. Like their human counterparts, they beat the crap out of the birds who claimed a legitimate North American heritage, spread diseases, stole nesting sites, ate everything in sight, and pooped some more.

From one hundred birds to a present-day total of over two hundred million.

At one point, the Department of Agriculture issued a recipe for starling pie.

It didn't catch on. I guess because it would be like eating a relative or something.

Standing at my window—my office perk—I toss the bag of pistachios back and forth between my hands and look at the starlings huddled on the ledge outside the frosty glass. Their feathers are fluffed against the cold, and the sunshine turns their black wings into spots of purple, pink, blue, and gray. One starling throws back his head and lets fly with a song faintly reminiscent of Kenny's singing. The starling next to him grabs the feathers on the back of the singer's neck.

The window erupts into black wings as the starlings fall from the ledge in a lemminglike wave. Only they land in the safety net of the trees lining the streets.

"Wichita?"

I turn around and see Janet—the museum's security guard—standing in my doorway. "Hi," I say.

She comes in and closes the door. "I was wondering . . . I mean, I have a question. And I thought maybe you could help me."

I try hard not to sigh. Those few hours of cramped sleep didn't prepare me for this. I wonder who I'm supposed to be today. Yesterday it was Ralph Lauren. Last week I was a combo special: The woman from *Ask Amy* and a father confessor, all on the same plate. Today I might have to grow a beard and change my name to Sigmund. Freud, that is.

Janet adjusts her Batman belt and gun, then sits down in the chair Jonz refused to occupy. "What do you think of these earrings?" she asks.

Ah. Ralph Lauren.

I look at the earrings. Nearly squeeze a few pistachios to death inside their crackling cellophane bag. Ralph Lauren never had to deal with this. The earrings are square, purple, maze-shaped things. They droop down to Janet's shoulders. "Nice," I say.

"You think? Do they go with the uniform?"

Brown duck and purple mazes.

I shrug, reluctant to piss off a woman carrying a firearm. "Um—"

"They don't, do they?"

"I'm not real good at this sort of thing."

"Do you think Kenny will like them?"

"Kenny?" Is this about relationships? I mentally grope in my persona bag for Dr. Ruth, Dr. Laura . . . *someone.*

"I was just wondering . . ." She clears her throat. Her shoes squeak on the floor as she moves around in the chair. "About . . . Kenny."

Kenny. Last week it was—

"What about Timothy?" I ask. "I thought—"

She waves a hand, and I catch a glimpse of more jewelry. A purple ring to match the earrings. "I think he's gay."

"He's not gay."

"He said he was gay."

Timothy is not gay. But I nearly ruined his escape route just now. He'd kill me if he found out. "Um . . . Guess I was wrong."

Janet giggles. "Bad gaydar, huh?"

"What?"

"Gaydar. You know." She twists the gun holster again. "I figured it out right off. That Timothy was gay."

I nod and decide to ignore the contradictions. "Uh-huh."

Silence. She scratches her shoulder and the rasp of fingernails on cloth echoes off the walls. "It must be the time of the month," she says finally. "I'm feeling horny."

I smile. The smile feels sick. A terminal patient wheeled out into the sunlight.

"Heck," she continues, "if you and Jonah weren't so tight, I'd be after him."

The terminal patient coughs and dies.

"Are those pistachios?" Janet asks.

I manage a nod. Then give her the bag.

"Thanks. I'm going to see if I can find Kenny." She stops at the door and turns back to me. "I think he's got a great sense of humor, don't you? The latest *Cosmo* said that humorous men are good in bed."

"Right. Sure."

She lays one hand along the gun and pats it. "A gal needs more than one kind of gun, you know."

Down, Freud.

Then she leaves, taking my pistachios with her.

I hope Kenny carries mace along with his humor.

Outside the window, the starlings wheel past, casting a shadow across my desk.

"I swear I'm going to poison them," Mom said one March morning eleven years ago. "Just look at them! They're everywhere."

I looked out the kitchen window at the carpet of starlings and thought about how I was two months away from leaving this town. Two months away from having enough money to buy something with four wheels that would get me past Hove's city limits. "They're just doing what nature told them to do," I said.

"They're in my martin houses again," Mom said.

"You never get any martins."

"And that," she pointed toward the stub-tailed body squeezing straw into the white gourd hanging from a pole, "that is why. I'm going to poison them."

"Maybe they want to poison you," I said. "All you ever do is rip apart their homes. You drag all their straw and grass out and throw it on the ground."

Mom's fingers squeezed the edge of the sink. "I'm not the home wrecker around here," she said.

It was the only time she ever mentioned Dolores.

The starlings wheel past my window. A black cloud. I watch their arcing flight and dream about curling up in the fleece blankets on my bed. Only my bed is occupied. The dream fizzles, and I wonder if I can get away with a cigarette . . . if the window isn't painted shut.

I'm tugging halfheartedly on the window frame when the phone rings.

"You don't have anything but tofu and Cap'n Crunch," Geena says when I answer.

"There's milk," I say.

"Skim. Yuck."

"Try the doughnut shop down the street."

"I don't like doughnuts."

"What do you like?"

"I don't know."

"Make yourself a PBJ. There's peanut butter in one of the cupboards."

"I don't like peanut butter."

I imagine myself grabbing the feathers on the back of her neck and shaking her.

It feels good.

"Go downstairs, turn right, and walk two blocks to the convenience store," I say out loud, after spitting the mental feathers out of my mouth. "Then you can have whatever you want."

"Don't you guys ever shop for groceries?"

"Only on alternating Tuesdays when the moon is full."

"What?"

"Never mind. Happy food hunting." And I hang up. Before I can reach down the wires and strangle the little bitch.

The phone rings again.

"You're just like Mom," Geena says. "You even sound like her. All whiney. Like this, *'Wanh, wanh, wanh.'*"

She hangs up.

I stare at the phone. This is sixteen? Did I act like this when I was sixteen?

And I am *not* my mother.

"I'm not the home wrecker around here," Mom said, her white knuckles bony under the skin.

I reached into the cupboard for one of the free Burger King glasses I had brought home from work and poured some water for a drink. "So leave," I said. "You have feet."

"Don't get snotty with me," she said. "I don't need snotty from you."

I walked away. Something I knew Mom would never do.

I am *not* my mother.

I know how to walk.

Jonz sticks his head into my office. "What's with Janet?" he asks, as if we never had the silent conversation earlier this morning.

"She's horny."

His face twitches. An involuntary combination of fear and revulsion.

"She took my pistachios," I say, but I'm not really thinking about the green nuts. I'm thinking about what Geena said.

"Ready for lunch?" Jonz asks.

I blink. "Not really. I . . . didn't get much sleep last night."

"Since when does exhaustion affect *your* appetite?"

"Since Geena showed up pregnant," I mutter.

Two emotions sizzle across his brain waves. I can feel them, even though his face is blank. The first emotion is surprise. The second is . . . a mongrel. A mixed breed of sadness and fear with just a dash of jealousy. Because I shut him out again.

I pay special attention to the stapler on my desk.

"I take it she wasn't anywhere near Hove when she called," he says, hiding the emotions he knows he can't hide.

"Joliet, actually," I say.

"And pregnant?"

"With Daddy in tow."

"Ah. The mysterious Dylan."

I nod.

"Come on," he says. "Lunch will help."

Lunch won't help.

If I know how, why don't I walk? Why don't I stop being a starling and start living another life? Like maybe the life of a solitary vireo. I like the sound of that. Flitting through the woods. Singing something beautiful. Alone. Proud. Free.

No pecking, no squabbling, no songs wheezing like a broken accordion, no angry feelings. No more collective memory unconscious. No more joined at the hip. No more Siamese twins.

Just me.

Maybe you can't walk.

I look down at my desk and see the white bones of my knuckles sticking up through the backs of my hands. Very carefully, I let go of the desk.

"No," I say standing up. "I'm not my mother."

Jonah's eyebrows disappear into his hair. "No one said you were."

But Geena did.

I just did.

I put on my coat and leave my thoughts behind. I'm tired. I can walk tomorrow. *Mañana.* There's always tomorrow.

Bundled up to the eyes, we head down to the hot dog stand on the corner. The man charring up pig flesh on the open grill looks like he might be a cannibal.

"Do you think he eats out of a trough in the mornings?" Jonz whispers as we wait in line. It's a running joke among the regulars.

"Undoubtedly."

But despite his hoggish appearance, the vendor has the right idea. We'll all stand out here for a hot dog if the hot dog is good enough. And he gets the jump on the summer business. No fair-weather-friend kind of vendor in the know would bother to set up shop on this corner.

"Twenty-five cents extra for those jalapeños," the vendor says to me.

Unless that fair-weather vendor gave extras for free.

"Thanks," I tell him. " 'You're a real friend. Not like some.' "

Just call me the sarcastic Eeyore.

The piglet eyes twitch. "If you don't like it, you can always go somewhere else." Then he doubles over at his own joke.

"Right."

Battling the wind, Jonz and I walk to our usual bench. The starlings have pooped on it.

"You'd think, given the number of hot dog buns I've given them, they'd be more grateful," Jonz says.

"Maybe they don't like hot dog buns."

I'm halfway through my lunch when my stomach rebels. Thoughts are never obedient. They come back when you don't want them, can't deal with them. I wrap up the leftover hot dog and hand it to Jonah.

"Not hungry?"

I shrug. Watch the starlings fight over some forgotten treasure in the brown grass.

"Do you think starlings ever get tired of each other?" I ask.

He's silent for long seconds. Trying to figure out what I really mean.

"Probably," he says. But he says it like someone might say, "And so on." Indicating the end of a sentence. The end of an argument.

I pretend not to notice when he throws away two uneaten hot dog remains.

Chapter 7

"Put that out!" I say as I walk into my apartment.

Geena blows a long train of smoke up toward the ceiling. "Why? Don't you smoke?"

I slam the door. "Sometimes. But I'm not pregnant. Didn't they show you any of those movies about what smoking does to a baby?"

She leans over and puts the cigarette out. "I don't remember." But her voice has lost the belligerence.

I shrug out of my coat and hang it on the wooden tree by the door before opening a window to let some fresh—relatively speaking—air into the place. "Where's Dylan?"

"He went out to get us some pizza," she says, thumbing through one of India's magazines.

"What about all that food I bought?" Call me an idiot, but I pretended it was an alternate, full-moon Tuesday and stopped by the grocery store yesterday.

"I don't like vegetables." She holds up the magazine. "Do you believe in horoscopes?"

"No," I say, sitting down across from her and wondering how to bring up the subject of pregnancy and healthy eating. Not to mention the virtues of not pissing off your free ride by being a complete—

"It says, 'You will have new adventures.'"

I'm still thinking about vegetables. And homicide. Or is that sorori-cide? Sister murder. "I could use some adventure," I say around my evil thoughts. Maybe my adventure will include a trip to Mexico to hide out from the law.

"That's my horoscope, not yours."

"Oh." Nix the Mexican adventure. For me, anyway. "Lucky you. Look, maybe you should—"

"Your horoscope says, 'You are a fickle lover and you will lose a friend.'" She laughs. "You're right. This thing is worthless."

"You should eat vegetables," I say, talking on autopilot.

"I'll eat all of the mushrooms," she says. "Dylan hates mushrooms."

I have my mouth opened to explain the difference between green, leafy stuff and fungi, when India and Dylan breeze into the room. Dylan looks sheepish.

"I found him wandering the streets," India says.

"All the buildings around here look the same," he says at the same time.

"Oh, good," India says before Geena can say anything—and Geena definitely was about to say something to Dylan. Probably something about installing a personal GPS. "I love that magazine. Read my horo-scope, will you? Taurus."

Geena shuts her mouth and looks down at the magazine in her lap. "'Fear not. Life is good.'"

"Not again," India moans. "Couldn't I have a failed love affair just *once*?"

"I'm the one with a failed love affair," I say.

"No," Geena says. "You're just a *fickle* lover. You're a *failure* at being a friend."

Dylan opens the pizza box and hands India a slice of pizza. "Wichita?" he asks, holding out a slice dripping grease and cheese. My stomach flops like a half-dead fish, but I take the slice.

"Thanks."

"Did you remember the paper?" Geena asks Dylan.

"Yeah." He tosses a copy of the *Tribune* to her. She hunts until she finds whatever it is she's looking for. Not mushrooms. She's picked all of those off the pizza and dropped them back into the box. Maybe they were too fresh.

"What are you looking for?" India asks around a mouthful of cheese.

"A movie," says Geena. "We're bored."

I want to tell her she's welcome to go be bored somewhere else rather than using up the hot water and filling my apartment with smoke and makeup and Dylan and hair spray—I can't believe people still *use* hair spray. I thought the sticky crap disappeared along with CFCs and the aerosol can. Maybe it was revitalized by the pump bottle.

"I'm going over to Chad's for the night," India says to me, knocking the hair spray thoughts off my mental dresser.

I know what she's saying. It's a subtle hint. Chad is India's in-between-real-relationships relationship. That is, he belches after downing a can of soda, he leaves his socks in the cracks of the sofa cushions, and he enjoys a rousing evening watching the WWE.

Definitely not real relationship material. At least not for India.

And she never spends the night.

Unless there's no hot water.

I nod and raise my piece of pizza in a salute to her subtlety. "Can you drop me off at The Club since the lovebirds are going out?"

She nods.

"We won't be back until late," Geena says. "The only good movie is at midnight. Can I have a key?"

Fear not. Life is good.

I wish I'd been born a Taurus instead of a Gemini.

• • •

"Do you believe in God?" Jonah asked me late one night during the hot summer when we were thirteen. We were lying on the grass in the middle of the football field.

I looked up at the stars. "I don't know," I said. "Mom says the sky is a blanket with holes in it, and the stars are light shining through from heaven."

He snorted. "You believe that?"

"No."

"The stars are flaming gas balls," he said.

"I know that, stupid. But Mom's going to church again."

"Oh. Sorry."

He wasn't sorry Mom was going to church, he was sorry I had to go with her. Every few years during the seventeen I lived at home, Mom would decide to turn her life around by trying a new version of religion. Sunday school was the inevitable result. Not for Mom. For me. Being thirteen is bad. Doing Sunday school lessons on Saturday night is worse. Having to wear a dress and sit in a cramped room with boys who—

"They comb their hair," I said.

"Who?"

"The boys in my Sunday school class."

"Oh." In the clumps of weeds under the bleachers, a cicada rasped a time or two, then began an uneven, singsong hum. "Do you believe in God, though?" Jonz asked again.

I stared up at the Big Dipper. "Do you think God is like a horoscope?"

He chewed on a piece of grass. I could almost hear him thinking. "No. Horoscopes tell you what's going to happen. God tells you what to do. Although I guess he tells you what's going to happen if you're bad."

"Sort of like when your mom threatens—"

"Yeah," he interrupted. "Like that."

"I don't think I'd like God very much," I said. "If I met him."

I'm going to The Club out of habit. I'm still on autopilot. India is silent as she drives. I don't know if she's thinking about her need for hot water and having to stay with Chad or my need to grow a backbone and tell my sister and Dylan that they can't sleep all day, stay out all night, and live free until they're ready for the nursing home.

"I know they just got here . . ." India begins.

My need to grow a backbone.

". . . but maybe they could make some plans?"

"I'll talk to Geena tomorrow," I say.

She stops the car outside The Club. Her heater doesn't work, and our breath is fogging up the windshield. I swipe at my side of the glass.

"I don't want to sound like a bitch or anything," she says. "It's just . . . crowded."

"I know. I'll talk to Geena." I start to get out—she's double parked—then I stop. "How do they separate Siamese twins?"

She purses her lips. "I don't know. A scalpel?"

I nod as if this were profound. "Thanks."

The Club is warm. Compared to the interior of India's car, anyway. It's the middle of the week, and not enough of the booths are filled with bodies to heat the place up. And that means I'll be cold again as soon as my cheeks thaw and my nose stops running. Up on the stage, there's a three-piece blues band. The Shy Boys. At least that's the name painted on the bass drum. Looking around, I see Jonah sitting in our usual place.

The guitarist leans in toward the microphone. "Won't at least some of you come and dance? We're dying up here. Can't you see we're shy? Come on, make us feel better."

Great. Pity as sales pitch.

I walk over to Jonah and toss my coat onto the opposite bench. He jumps, and I catch the tail end of something in his eyes. A black hole. An empty black hole in his eyes. And it's worse than gravity and it's grabbing me and sucking me down. . . . And I say the first stupid thing to come into my head.

"Want to dance? The Shy Boys are making me feel guilty."

He blinks, and the black hole winks out in a quirk of his lips. "Are you kidding? I look like an idiot when I dance."

"It's a slow song. All you have to do is shuffle around. Pretend I'm a walker and you're ninety or something."

He shakes his head, but he slides out of the booth.

"All *right!*" says the guitarist as we walk up to the stage. "Thanks, folks."

"I'm a folk," I say to Jonah, trying to pretend I'm not shaking. "You're a folk."

He looks at me funny, but I step into his arms and lay my cold cheek against his shirt. And I step into the scents of Tide and deodorant soap and . . . Jonah. A combination of smells I've known almost since I knew what a smell *was*. It's all tied up with grass and stars and hot upstairs rooms and Burger King . . . and we're both shuffling somewhat in time to whatever music the three-piece is playing.

Then Jonz lets out a breath—the first time he's used his lungs since I touched him. I can feel his chest fall and rise under my cheekbone. For several bars he simply rests his chin on the top of my head as we drift back and forth in a kind of drowsy rectangle. I'm almost asleep—too worn out to realize I'm too comfortable drifting like this—when he drops his lips to my ear and his breath moves my hair.

"Do you believe in God?" he asks.

"I don't think I'd like God very much," I said into the cicada-noisy night. "If I met him."

"Why not?" Jonz asked. "I mean, what if he only punished bad people?"

61

"But Job wasn't bad. I think God just likes being mean. I'd rather have a horoscope."

"All that stuff is just made up."

"No, it isn't." I pointed up toward the stars. "It's based on them."

"They're just stars. They don't do a thing."

I wasn't ready to give up just yet. "The moon does stuff to the ocean. Why can't the stars do stuff to people?"

"Yeah. Right. It's all made up. See, I'll tell you your future."

I rolled over onto my stomach. This was interesting. Jonah the oracle. "Okay."

He grabbed my hand and rolled his eyes back into his head. "We'll be friends until we die—"

"That's it? I already knew that."

"—and Filthy Jeff will say 'hi' to you all next year." He let go of my hand.

"That sucked. You're as bad as that lady who writes the one in the paper. 'Venus rising in Capricorn' or something like that."

"Yeah? Well, at least mine will come true."

I punched him in the arm.

"Do you believe in God?" Jonah whispers into my ear.

I lean back. But I can't look any higher than the pulse in his throat. Such a tiny thing. Blood flowing with each beat. Mike must have turned up the heat. It's summer hot in here. And somewhere under the stage, a cicada starts to hum.

No, it's an amplifier. And it's smoking.

"Ah, shit," the guitarist says. "Hey, Mike? You got a fire extinguisher?"

We'll be friends until we die.

I've been going about this all wrong. You can't *drift* away from a friend.

Siamese twins don't drift. One twin can't decide to get up off the couch on Saturday and say, "See you later," and walk out the door. You can't drift. You need . . .

A scalpel.

I pull out of Jonah's arms and walk back to the booth.

Jonah follows me.

"I'm tired," I say.

I'm scared.

I swallow. Try again. "I'm . . . tired, and it's . . ."

I'm scared I'll become my mother.

"It's just that . . ."

I don't want to make the mistakes my parents made. I don't want to spend my life fighting over pancakes and—

—hurting you. Or me.

He frowns. "Want to call it quits?"

I blink. The moment of truth.

Too soon, too soon.

Fear tastes like the rusty bars on the merry-go-round.

"If you want to go home now, that's fine with me."

Home. Do I want to go home. To India. Geena. Dylan.

He isn't handing me a scalpel.

"I . . . sure," I mumble. "Yeah."

No.

No, this isn't what I want at all. Why can't he understand me? How can he know I'm thinking about pistachios, but he can't know what I mean—

And it hits me.

Because he doesn't want to know.

Somehow, I've put on India's exercise weights. My wrists are heavy on the table and my ankles feel thick and bulky. And maybe she gets her heart rate up with a weight that straps around her chest. I'm wearing that one, too.

"You go on," I say. "I think . . . I think I want a cup of coffee."

He already has his coat on and he's looking down at me. "Fine," he says. Nothing more.

I hold my breath.

"See you tomorrow," he says.

And the casual words sound like the words he must have said when he climbed out of the green Volvo.

I barely feel the cold air as the door swings shut behind him.

I think I believe in God. I just don't want to meet him.

Jonah didn't leave me on the merry-go-round. Even after I threw up on him. It was tomato soup and carrots. Mom was going through a beta-carotene phase. Jonah just stared at his shirt until I started to cry.

"Hey, it doesn't matter," he said. He stopped the merry-go-round, then took off his flannel shirt and buried it in the sand. "I was sick the first time," he said, shivering because a T-shirt in the northern, early-September breeze wasn't nearly enough protection.

I sat on the edge of the merry-go-round. Completely humiliated. "I'm sorry," I said, sniffing hard. "I didn't mean to."

"You threw up," he said. "No one means to throw up. Except for my dog. I think he enjoys it."

I sniffed again. "You have a dog?" I wanted a dog. Any kind of dog. Even a wiener dog. Well, maybe not a poodle. Just a dog. Poodles weren't really dogs.

"Yeah. You want to see him? After school, I mean."

I nodded. "But what about your shirt?"

He smiled his missing-teeth grin. "You want to wear it?"

"Yuck."

"So leave it."

"Did your friend leave?"

I'm shivering. I look up and find Mike sitting across from me. "Yeah."

"I'm sorry about the fire."

"The what?"

He frowns. "The fire. Up on stage?"

"Oh. Right. No problem."

His fingers drum on the table. "You okay?"

I nod. "Sure."

More drumming. "Maybe . . . maybe you'd like . . . I mean . . ." He takes a deep breath. "Would you like to go out for a cup of coffee or something?" He looks down at the nearly empty cup on the table and blushes. Mutters. It sounds like "stupid," but I don't know for sure.

I look at him. Really look at him. Look past the hair and asceticism. And I see a white surgical table. Spotlights. Masked nurses. Gleaming rows of instruments made for cutting. All bright and clean and sharp.

"Sure," I say. "I'd like that."

Chapter 8

One night, I woke up cold and wet. I'm not sure how old I was, but I could barely see over the top of the kitchen table. Which means the wet bed wasn't a pleasant place to be. Water had nothing to do with it. Music floated into my room, carried on the light showing through the crack under the door. Struggling out from under the covers, I pushed off my pajama bottoms and followed the music. If I found the music, I would find Mom, and while she might be angry about the bed, she'd fix everything.

The light and music came from downstairs. Stairs were still tricky—especially at night—so I put both hands flat against the wall and reached one bare toe for the shadowed step. Under my palms, the wall felt cool and pebbly from the bubbles the paint roller had left behind. The music sounded softer here on the stairs than it had coming under my bedroom door. A soft country-style jazz. I slid my hands along the painted wall, felt for the steps, and felt goose bumps crawl up my bare legs.

Downstairs, the coffee table had been pushed up tight against the couch, and in the vacant space, Mom and Dad were dancing in the light and music. Mom's cheek rested against Dad's shoulder. She was facing me, but her eyes were closed and a smile I couldn't remember touched the corners of her lips. I opened my mouth to call to her, but I never got to say a word.

Dad reached up and caught her wrists. His knuckles white around her bones, he stepped back. "What are you trying to do, Maggie?" he asked.

"I'm dancing, Brad. What does it look like?"

His face twisted, and he threw her wrists away—pushed them away from him and dropped them. "Don't play that game with me."

"I'm *not!*"

But he'd already turned his back on her. I shrank into the shadows. Even at kitchen-table height, I knew I wasn't welcome here. Dad walked past me. I don't think he saw me at all. From the living room, I could hear tears mix with the music.

Hands against the wall, I climbed back up each step until I reached the safety of my bedroom. I spent the rest of the night curled up in a ball of blankets at the foot of my bed. Shivering.

"It's cold tonight," Mike says as we walk into the wind. A few painful steps farther and he adds, "I'm sorry I don't have a car."

"I don't have one, either," I say through the ice forming on my scarf.

"They make great coffee. This shop. And it's warmer than my place." He laughs a short, shivery laugh.

My laugh sounds cold in return.

The shop may make great coffee, but it's closed. At least, that's what the sign on the door says. CLOSED FOR REPAIRS. Mike cups his hands next to the glass and peers inside the shop, vainly looking for signs of life. He gives up and shifts from foot to foot.

His embarrassment tastes like alum. My mouth shrivels.

Or maybe it's the taste left from the memory of Mom's tears and the look on my father's face as he threw away her smile.

It's up to me to walk away.

End it before it goes as far as the living-room dance floor.

I am not my mother.

I swallow, press my hands against the stairway wall, and stretch my toe, feeling for that first step.

"Look," I say, "we could go to my apartment. I can't guarantee good coffee, but maybe if you make it? My roommate says my coffee tastes like something you'd find under a bus."

Mike stops shifting and gives me a big, lost-puppy smile.

We take the bus. Make polite, casual talk. But polite, casual words can't remove my unsteadiness as I lean against the wall and wonder where—what—the next step is.

"This is a nice place," Mike says after I open the door.

"It's crowded," I tell him. "My sister and her . . . friend are here for a bit."

He looks around.

"They're at a movie."

"Oh, really?"

"The kitchen's this way." Which is a ridiculous thing to say since the kitchen is more than obvious. You can't miss it.

I point to the top cupboard. "The coffee's up there."

"Okay," Mike says.

I smile at him and realize—maybe the light is better up here—that he's shaved and he might, just might, have had a haircut. It's hard to tell since he's got his long hair dragged into a ponytail.

He smiles back. "I can take over from here," he says. "I know how to do the rest."

"I know how to do the rest," Jonah said, stirring the pot on the stove.

I looked at him out of the sides of my eyes. "Oh, puh-leeze," I said. "You haven't added any sugar."

We were making cocoa. Jonz was sixteen and adult and full of disdain for instant coffee. And instant coffee was the only thing Mom kept in the cupboard. She said it was because she needed instant dipping sauce when the Pecan Sandies called to her at night. I think it might have been because Dad was too cheap to buy her a coffeemaker. Unfortunately, the instant part of Mom's life didn't extend to cocoa. That was made the old-fashioned way: milk, sugar, cocoa, and a stove.

"It's just cocoa," Jonz said. "Little kids drink it." He looked at me as if to point out that I was still fifteen.

"It's just coffee," Mike says, laughing.

I blink and smile. I'm smiling a lot. "It's good."

"Smile on the outside and you'll smile on the inside." Mom's maxim. Given to me the day she left me outside the elementary school for the first time.

"Thanks," Mike says.

"It's better than your beer."

"I'm not sure if I'm supposed to say 'thanks' again or not," he says, pretending to frown.

When he laughs, his eyes don't scrunch. But his laugh comes from inside of him. I can't connect him with all those times I've heard "All Along the Watchtower" in The Club. He doesn't seem like the kind of guy women leave. More like the kind they marry and have six kids with.

"How come you're not married?" I ask him.

He laughs again. "I was."

"And?"

"Never again."

"That bad?"

"Worse."

I wonder if they slow-danced.

I get up, go into the living room, and find the magazine. "What's your sign?" I say to him.

"I'm not sure. Pisces, I think."

I look down at the magazine. Under Pisces I read: *Watch your back, Pisces.*

"What's it say?" Mike asks.

" 'Fear not. Life is good,' " I say.

"Figures," he says. "All that stuff is just made up."

"All that stuff is just made up," Jonz said. "See, I'll tell you your future."

I rolled over—

"Probably," I say to Mike, dropping the magazine and memory onto the coffee table. I desperately want a cigarette. I've made it all day. I've been good. What is one more cigarette going to do to me? If I quit smoking tomorrow instead of today, what difference will it make to the future of my lungs?

I reach for the pack, only—

"Isn't this what you're supposed to be doing with Morgan?" I asked.

"It's what I'm doing with you," Jonz said.

—my fingers hover above the pack, then I let my hand fall against my thigh.

"My ex always read her horoscope," Mike is saying. "She had all these crystals and shit. Always going on about some kind of religion or other."

I walk back to the kitchen, lean on the door frame, and look at him.

Jonz is in my head. I'm a goddamn Gemini.

"*A scalpel?*" India says in my head.

"Mike . . ." I begin. Then I give up and kiss him.

"Whoa!" Mike says as he pulls back. "Is my coffee that good?"

I laugh a little, embarrassed at myself.

"You kissed him, didn't you?" Jonah asked after Filthy Jeff brought me home. Jonah had tossed a few rocks at my window and asked for the post-dance report.

"No." A total lie. Filthy Jeff had shuffled and asked, and I had wanted to find out what it felt like to kiss a guy.

Sort of damp.

I wasn't sure what all the fuss was about.

Jonz looked at me, then shook his head. "You kissed him."

I laugh a little, embarrassed at myself for wanting Jonah out of my head so bad I would take advantage of Mike.

"Yeah," I say, "your coffee is a spiritual experience."

Mike fakes surprise, swirling the coffee around in his cup. "Forget bear balls," he says. "I'll just bottle this and sell it as an aphrodisiac."

I try to keep laughing. I want to sink through the floor and down into the apartment underneath mine, but I think it's inhabited by an elderly couple with two or three illegal chihuahuas. Which might make the situation worse, not better. *"Looky here, Mildred. A red-faced ignoramus. And it's done gone and scared little Fido, Fluffy, and Killer."*

Mike looks up and smiles.

"You kissed him," Jonah said.

"Did not."

"Sure did. You smell different."

I rolled my eyes. "I smell like stinky cologne. We danced, okay?"

"You kissed him." Jonz leaned forward. "Your mouth smells like cologne, so unless you've been drinking it . . ."

For some reason, I was holding my breath. Jonz was too close and it felt funny. My stomach turned warm. Whiskey warm. And I should know.

I had snuck some out of the bottle hidden in Dad's desk drawer just the other day.

I jerked back. "Did not."

Jonz laughed, but his eyes didn't scrunch.

I look down at Mike and all I can see is a smiling scalpel.

Maybe if . . .

I kiss him again.

It's not exactly a seduction scene. You know what I mean. The kind you see in movies. Someone goes over to the CD collection and puts on one of those slow-moving songs. Someone lights a candle. Two someones do the hesitant tango on the couch. That kind of seduction scene.

We're on the couch, but that's about it. Everything is kind of clumsy. Mike has his arm along the back, but I'm not sure what to do with *my* arm. I kiss him. He kisses me. We bash noses until we figure out how not to get in each other's way.

I'm working on keeping my mind neutral. Concentrate on Mike. And coffee. And whether or not my nose is still cold from the walk home—

"Shit, it's cold here," Jonz said the first winter we spent in the wind tunnel of downtown Chicago. "I think my nose is frozen."

"You have to wrap your scarf. . . ." I pulled him to a stop. "Look, it's an early Christmas present, okay?" And I tugged the scarf I had just bought for him out of my bag and wrapped it around his lower face.

His eyes scrunched above the cream fake cashmere.

I push the mental image of Jonah away and mash my mouth tighter against Mike's. Mike doesn't seem to mind. He's rubbing my back with the hand that doesn't belong to the arm resting on the couch. I can feel his hand inch under my sweater until it's touching bare skin.

Bare skin. Bare skin will take us off the couch and into the room that still smells a little like unwashed teen body and smoke. Bare skin . . .

But you have to get to bare skin if you're going to make an incision.

Mike pulls back a little. "I don't normally do this on a first date," he says, sounding rueful.

"Me, either," I say, sounding desperate. "Do you want to go into the bedroom?"

He blinks and looks worried. All he knows about me is that I know a little something about the blues and that I get tired of "Watchtower." Oh, and I like his coffee, but he can't be sure about that since he just found out thirty minutes ago. For all he knows, I stick hat pins into guys or keep them chained up in my closet as permanent love slaves.

So I kiss him confident. Well, kiss him until he doesn't care, anyway.

"Sure," he says.

If the couch was awkward, the bedroom is downright unbearable. We avoid looking at each other as we tug off our winter shells. This takes longer than you would think, what with three shirts, jeans, socks . . . but somehow we end up on the bed in our underwear. The bed smells like stale cigarettes. I hope Mike doesn't notice.

I don't think he does.

He pulls my bra down and runs his tongue over my nipple. I squirm because it tickles—

"Cut it out!" I said to Jonz. I was sitting on the lower limb of the elm tree in his front yard. I'd climbed up there to prove that while I might puke at the sight of a spinning top, at least I wasn't scared of heights . . . like some people. Jonz responded by grabbing a piece of grass and dragging it across my bare foot, which was all he could reach.

"Cut it out. It tickles."

• • •

I scrunch my eyes shut and reach for Mike, pinning his face between my hands and pulling him up for a kiss. I'm feeling guilty and scared and excited and worried and embarrassed all at the same time. Is this normal? I don't know. Right now, I don't care.

Mike's hand slips down over my stomach and between my legs. My first reaction is to clamp my thighs together, but he kisses me and I relax, let him tease me until I'm past wet, past caring.

Then he rolls over and fumbles around for something on the floor. And I'm wondering why he's looking for dust bunnies *now*, when it hits me cold and nasty and unforgivable.

Protection.

Condom.

Idiot.

"You kissed him."

"Isn't this something you should be doing with her?"

"It's something I'm doing with you."

Mike pulls me on top of him, only I don't know what to do, so we roll back and he's between my legs and I didn't expect it to hurt this much.

And now maybe forgetting the condom is more forgivable.

Maybe it's possible to understand why I'm trying this particular scalpel to cut my Gemini life in half. This particular scalpel to cut me free and let me walk away from the rest of the starlings.

Yeah, you guessed it.

I am—*was*—the last surviving twenty-eight-year-old virgin.

Ch ap te r   9

How did this come to pass? Not the hairy bartender snoring in my bed. That is entirely my own doing, and I can trace the moments leading up to *that* from my careless magic wand comment (*"It can be used for good or evil"*) to the somewhat painful experience of a moment ago.

How did I come to be a twenty-eight-year-old virgin?

I'm not sure. It wasn't because of disease. Or danger. Or because I was waiting for just the right man. It certainly wasn't because of some political/religious campaign about the joys of abstinence.

It just . . . happened.

Usually because I found the male brain too dense for my lackluster (or bored) sex drive to overcome.

There was Filthy Jeff. He got in one damp kiss. After that, I managed to avoid the stage at the head of the cafeteria by a thousand ingenious methods, each more complicated than the last. One method actually involved my climbing in through the window of the girls' restroom while Jonah nabbed my things from my locker—

But that's another story.

Filthy Jeff got in one damp kiss.

Ben got in a hand on a naked breast.

Scott got a hand down into my underwear just before I hit him.

And Timothy—yes, Timothy my boss—and I had one heated hand-to-genital exchange the night we found out my superbly crafted grant proposal had nailed us the cash we needed to keep the museum afloat.

But we were both drunk on champagne and success, and we were both really very sorry the next day.

We haven't mentioned it since.

And that is the extent of my hands-on sexual experience. Excluding tonight, of course.

My experiences with the density of the male brain . . . Well, that would take a lot longer, and the list of thick heads would look a little like the "Naughty Boys" list that Santa keeps. If I could even remember the names that correspond with the density.

But *what* does not really explain *why*.

I don't know why.

Maybe I don't *want* to know why.

Something hits my window.

I'm half asleep, so my eyelids bounce and my heart thumps with the usual "something goes bump in the night" bounce and thump.

Thuck.

Stone on glass.

I can feel sweat trickling down my side, just under my rib cage.

"What the hell?" Mike mutters.

Thuck.

"Just some kids," I say into my pillow. The sweat catches on the edge of my stomach, forms a ticklish pool, then whispers on down to the sheet.

Thuck.

Mike rolls out of bed. I can hear him fumble with the curtain and the latch. Gray city light pours into the room as he pushes the curtain out of his way.

Thuck.

The window slides up. "Hey!" Mike yells. "Fuck off." He slams the window down and the curtain falls back, turning the room dark. The bed dips a little as he climbs back in. He rubs my arm. "Some guy," he says. "He took off."

I believe in God. I just don't want to meet him.

Just past the sign that reads WELCOME TO HOVE, POPULATION 4,300—seasonally altered by a rival football team and some spray paint to read, WELCOME TO SHIT HOLE—stood a windmill, the last remnant of the farm that existed before the town spread east. The base of the windmill was a complex crisscross of wood-and-metal bracing. Some of the wood had rotted through, and climbing up to the round circle of blades and painting your name in a prominent place had become the dare of choice. The June after I found Jonz and Morgan rocking the green Volvo, I dared myself to climb up and paint my name.

I made Jonah go with me.

"You're crazy," he said, looking up twenty-five feet of old wood and rusty metal. "You're not climbing up that."

"Watch me." I tucked the mini spray can I had bought specially for the occasion into the pocket of my shorts. I had climbed past two crisscrosses when Jonz grabbed my ankle.

"Cheetah . . ."

"It'll be okay," I said, grinning down at him.

I didn't actually think it would be okay. But for some reason, ever since he'd handed me that cigarette, I'd had the feeling that no one would remember me. I was just a shadow—forgotten once the substance is gone. And sometime late the night before, I'd had the ingenious idea of putting my name on the windmill. Not on the blades, on the tail.

Putting your name on the blades meant you never had to let go of the base. You just reached up with one hand and sprayed your name on the nearest blade—whichever one the wind had left in the lowest position—then you climbed back down. The tail was different. To reach it, you had to actually climb up onto the rotten upper platform and pull the tail toward you.

Jonah thought I was going for a blade. If he'd known what I was planning, he would have tied me to a tree until the mood passed.

I looked back down. Jonz was looking up at me. His face had turned several shades of green. Darker with each crisscross I passed.

"You'd better shut your eyes or stop looking," I said.

Jonz shook his head. "You're gonna fall."

I reached for the crisscross above my head. "Then you'll hear my body hit the ground," I said, "so you don't need—"

The sound of Jonah puking in the bushes nearby interrupted me.

"I told you not to look," I said when the retching stopped.

No answer.

I looked down again. Usually, looking down didn't make me dizzy, but I wasn't used to Jonah looking back up. He seemed farther away like that. I covered the bad spinning feeling with a grin. "Trust me," I said. "I'm fine."

"Trust me. She's just the type of person to kick us out."

I jerk awake, disoriented, dangling from a windmill.

It's Geena and Dylan.

"C'mon, Wichita," Geena says, but her voice is coming from the other side of the bed.

"What're you shaking me for?" Mike mumbles.

Geena screams.

And keeps screaming.

"Jesus," Mike says, pulling the blanket over his ears. "It's my ex."

I sit up, completely forgetting the standard state of nudity. Dylan gulps. I yank up the sheet. "*Geena!* Shut up!" I say, just loud enough to cut through the scream. Which is pretty loud.

Geena shuts up. The screaming part, anyway.

"Oh," she says. Then, "What the hell are you doing in our bed?"

I look around the room, pretending to see it for the first time. "What? Isn't this my room? Am I in the wrong apartment?"

"You had *sex* in *our BED?*" Geena appears to be lacking a sarcasm gene. She must have inherited that particular hole in her DNA from Mom.

"Uh . . . Geena," Dylan says. "Maybe we should let them get dressed. Or something."

Or something is right.

I'm not feeling particularly friendly or even decent, so I grab the blanket at the foot of the bed and wrap it around me.

"C'mon," I say to the cute couple. "Living room."

Behind me, I hear Mike fumble around for his clothes. This little event is embarrassing, but it's not as bad as it would have been if I'd woken up with my alarm tomorrow and found Mike in my bed. What do you say to someone at six thirty A.M.? "Hey, nice butt. Glad I could meet you like this"?

I shiver under the blanket.

In movies, the girl always gets out of bed and throws a shawl over herself so she can leave her lover all cozy while she pads around in PG-13-rated glory to look at the moon or do some other sappy activity. The shawl stays put. This blanket isn't as cooperative. It keeps sliding down off my shoulder, and when I wrap it ball gown–style over my boobs it just falls off completely. I make it to the easy chair without tripping and without giving Dylan more than he's already seen. Not that it matters. He's seen all of my sister, and I'm just an older, saggier, genetic version, so big whoop-dee-do.

I sit down and wait for Geena and Dylan to sit on the couch. "It's my bed," I say, when they're firmly planted, "and it's in my apartment."

"Fuck you," Geena says. "We're leaving."

She stands up, but Dylan stays put.

"C'mon, Dylan."

"Uh . . . Geena?"

Does this guy begin every sentence with "Uh . . . Geena?" I look at my little sister's face. Not that I blame him.

"What?" Geena asks.

"I don't have any money."

Ah. The moment of truth.

Geena shrugs. "I've got some."

"No, you don't. You used it for the movie."

She bites her lip.

She sits back down.

Mike walks out of the bedroom. He absorbs the atmosphere. "Looks like you all will need some coffee," he says before heading into the kitchen.

We're still sitting in silence when he comes back into the living room. He leans down and gives me a kiss on the cheek. "Four's a crowd," he says. "Especially at family functions." He starts to say something more, then he shrugs. "See you round."

I smile around my embarrassment, my shame, my guilt—how could I not feel guilty?—and try to say something innocuous like "See you at The Club." But it sticks in my throat because it hits me that I might never go to The Club again. So I swallow innocuous and smile and nod and manage to mumble, "Thanks for the coffee."

He opens the door and leaves. Dylan's entire body is leaning after him.

"Too bad, kid," I say to Dylan. "You've mixed genes with Geena here, so I think you qualify as family."

He sinks back into the couch.

"How do you know it's Dylan?" Geena asks, folding her arms over her belly.

"Oh, should I be expecting someone else? Maybe he'll have some money and you can all move to the Regency. I hear they've got great room service."

"Fuck you," Geena says again.

The coffeepot gurgles.

"Dylan? Would you mind getting us some coffee?" I ask.

Dylan disappears fast enough to create a spinning action and turn me nauseated.

Looking down at Jonah, I could feel my head and stomach spin. I looked back up and the spinning stopped.

"You can reach the blade from there," he yelled.

"Right," I said as I hoisted myself up onto the platform.

"Cheetah! What the fuck are you doing?"

Down where Jonah stood, the windmill's blades made a happy croaking sound—like frogs in spring when the ponds thaw. Up at the top, the blades creaked and groaned and laughed—a metal girl who's just gotten ditched before the biggest party of the year. Laughing sadness. Laughing loneliness.

I didn't dare look down. Beneath me, the rotten boards made a crackling sound. Beneath the boards, Jonz was yelling . . . something. I reached for the tail and pulled it toward me. It stuck, then came free, nearly knocking me off and down, down, down.

I dug into my pocket for the mini can of spray paint. Popped the lid and let it drop. Down, down, down.

Jonah threw up again.

I shook the can. The boards cracked. I started to spray "Cheetah," then something changed my mind.

Wichita Gray.

In gold spray paint.

Partway back down, the crisscross brace I was holding on to broke. I fell ten feet and landed right on my back, right in front of Jonah.

"Ah, Jesus. Cheetah . . ." He dropped to his knees beside me.

I stared up at the windmill and tried to catch the wind that had been knocked out of me. A June breeze twisted off the hot ground and twirled the blades, moved the tail.

Wichita Gray.

"Look at my name," I said to Jonz. "I'm immortalized."

"Are you okay?" he asked, instead of looking.

"I'm fine. Trust me." And then I laughed.

"I thought we could trust you," Geena says, crossing her arms tight over her boobs.

Three cups of cold coffee sit on the coffee table. Make that two cups of cold coffee sit on the table. Dylan is playing with his cup. Swirling coffee around. Clockwise. Counterclockwise. Around and around. I want to tell him to put the damn mug back on the table and sit still, but he isn't doing anything wrong.

"Trust me for what?" I finally ask Geena. "Free room and board?"

"We've only been here *two days*," she says.

"Is that all?" I look around at the piles of dirty clothes, the almost-but-not-quite-empty pizza box, the discarded Coke cans.

Geena blushes.

"Sorry about the mess," Dylan says. "I'll pick it up right now."

"Sit down," I tell him. "You can both pick it up in a minute."

Geena's lower lip trembles. She looks just like Mom.

Mom's lower lip trembled. "You don't love me anymore," she said.

Dad dropped his newspaper. "Oh, for God's sake, Maggie. Can't you see I'm reading?"

The pancakes sat in the middle of the table.

A dribble of syrup ran down the side of the bottle, thick as tears.

"Eat your breakfast, Wichita," Mom said. "It will get cold."

It was already cold.

Geena's lip trembles. "You want me to freeze to death out in the alley."

To his credit, Dylan doesn't tell her he'll keep her warm. He just stares at me. What kind of monster would turn her sister out into an alley?

"I'm not going to make her sleep in the alley," I tell him. "Don't worry." I look at Geena's lip. "Cut it out with the lip, okay?"

The lip stops moving.

"Tonight you sleep in my bed. Tomorrow you look for a job. You find a job, then you start looking for an apartment." I feel like I should add "*Capice?*" to the end of the sentence. That's me. Wichita Gray. Capone henchman. Henchwoman. Henchperson?

"But I'm *pregnant*," Geena wails.

I stare at her. "Pregnant women work and have their own apartments," I say. "I know it's hard to believe, but I've actually seen it happen. Just last year, Dorothy, this woman at the museum? She had twins in the coffee room. Pretty exciting."

"And she wrapped them up in swaddling clothes and got back to work while carrying them on her back, right?" Geena says, doing a pretty good imitation of sarcasm.

"Hey, not bad," I say.

She tucks her hands back into the crooks of her arms. "I'm not sleeping in that bed," she says. "Not unless you change the sheets."

"Fine," I say. "You help."

We're pulling off the sheets when Geena notices the blood. There's not much, but it shows.

"Wow," she says, leaning closer. "What were you guys into?" She looks up at me. She can't miss the red on my face.

"You weren't—?" She starts laughing. "You know what's funny?" she asks, when she stops to catch her breath. "Mom's always telling me what a slut you were when you were my age."

The windmill blew down in a July storm right after Jonah and I left for Chicago.

Chapter 10

"You didn't have to do that," Jonz says.

My fingers squeeze the door frame of his office.

After the lovebirds went to bed, I spent the night on the couch. When India came home around five thirty A.M., I scared years off her life by not bothering to pretend I was sleeping. I wasn't sleeping because once Dylan and Geena disappeared into my room, the apartment settled into a state of thick, watchful guilt. Like the monster under the bed. Salivating and waiting until you close your eyes. Waiting to pounce. I closed my eyes and saw what I never saw. I saw Jonah's face as Mike slid open the window. So I stopped closing my eyes. And India coming through the door felt like having morning sunlight slide under the bed and torch the monster.

Only the monster still exists.

I didn't bother to stop by the coffee room at the museum.

I didn't bother to take off my coat.

I went to Jonah.

Caught myself on the door frame when I found him.

Betraying a lover is nothing compared to betraying a friend.

"You didn't have to do that," he says.

By "that" he means last night. Mike. The window.

My fingers squeeze the door frame.

Kenny's late this morning, and the hall is vacant of people and the morning noises people make when they show up at work. We're all alone and lonely.

"You could have just told me." His hands are resting on the arms of his squeaky chair. An old wooden, tilt-back chair. We rescued it from a Dumpster. Someone had thought it was useless. Jonah thought it was beautiful. Sandpaper. Paint remover. Varnish. We scraped and sanded that damn chair for a week of evenings before Jonz dubbed it clean enough for varnish. It never stopped squeaking, though. Not even an entire bottle of machine oil stopped the protest of a tired piece of furniture whenever the occupant so much as twitched.

"You could have just told me," Jonz says. He says it so quietly the chair doesn't make a noise.

I squeeze the door frame. Tighter.

"I don't know how to talk to you," I say, making excuses, still staring at his hands where they rest on the chair arms. "I don't know how to . . . talk."

"We talk," he says, lips twisting. "We just don't use words."

"And that's the problem, isn't it?" I say. "If we used words, I could have said something. But talking without words means you can ignore what I'm trying to say."

The chair cries in protest as Jonah's head jerks up.

"It's *my* fault?" he asks. And he doesn't mean Mike anymore. He means us. The distance growing between us.

"You didn't listen," I say.

"You didn't say anything."

"Yes, I did."

"You moped, you told me everything was just great, you shoved me off, you started smoking again, and now you've gone and fucked the bartender." He snorts. "Wonderful. Lots of meaningful content."

"Oh yeah? And you just sit around staring at me and frowning and scrunching up your face and doing nothing and saying nothing and pretending nothing's wrong—"

"I'm not the one who's pretending nothing's wrong."

"—and waiting for me to do something about it, because you *refuse* to hear anything I'm saying."

"You're not saying *anything!* All you did was fuck Mike. What's that say?"

"It says I want a scalpel," I say. Scream. Whatever.

He's watching my face, but his hands are hurting the arms of the rescued chair. At least they would be hurting the arms of the chair if human flesh were harder than the flesh of trees.

"It says I want away from you," I say. And I can barely hear the words as they come out of my mouth.

But he hears them. His hands let go of the chair.

"I want away from you," I say again.

He starts to laugh. The lonely metal sound of the old windmill in the winter wind. Like metal blades turning in a winter wind.

And I understand. Understand something I felt but never quite accepted.

"It's you!" I say. "I thought it was just me. Only it's you, too."

The skin covering his face stretches . . . stretches tight over the bones. "What do you mean?"

"It's not just me," I say, working it out as I fumble for words. "You want it to be . . . *different.* I thought this was all about me being . . . about me *not* being a damn bird. But it's you, too."

His hair falls down into his eyes. He's looking at the desk, but when he looks up at me . . . I can't feel the words. I can only feel what his eyes are saying. And what they're saying is so crazy and hot and burning and—

I push back hard. Push away from the door frame. Somehow, I'm still in the doorway, but I feel like I've pushed myself back, back, back through the wall behind me and deep into the future. I'm dipping Pecan Sandies and pecking, pecking, pecking at him, only he's running off to the Postmistress of Love. . . .

And I am not going to be my mother.

"No," I say, my voice a rusty squeak. "No. I don't want . . . I don't want fighting and hurting . . . each other and being . . . *common*. I want something . . . I don't want—"

He nods, cutting me off. "I think I've got that figured out."

I start to shake my head, because he's got it all wrong. I want to deny everything, tell him . . . But I've gone this far, I shouldn't have to bear all this guilt for nothing.

"Just go," he says.

I leave.

I feel like a piece of me has been cut off and I'm bleeding all over the hallway floor. . . . But that was the point of last night, wasn't it?

As I walk away, I hear fragile porcelain hit the wall of Jonz' office. I hear pieces skitter across the tile floor.

I walk to my office. It looks the same as when I left it yesterday. Outside the window, the sun is shedding golden grace on the glass and stone. But inside . . .

Still in my wool coat, I sit down. My chair doesn't squeak. It's standard issue. Just like everything else in this room. Leaning my elbows on the desktop, I press the heels of my hands into my eyes.

One of the strangest parts about Christianity is the Bible. The Bible is filled with all kinds of bizarre stuff. For example, there's a section that says something like, "If your eye causes you to sin, gouge it out. If your hand causes you to sin, cut it off." That's not a perfect quote. I'm not good at memorization. Something that lost me a lot of gold stars in Sunday school class. But my point is . . .

. . . I've gone and cut off half of *myself*. The Siamese twins are separated. Gemini have become Geminus and Geminus. It remains to be seen if I can live, breathe, and think as half a person.

No, that was a Freudian slip. I am a *whole* person. Jonz is a whole person. We are now going to function as individuals. In a way, I've done him a favor. He doesn't love me. Not like he thinks. He only thinks he loves me because he's so used to having me around. Now he can go find someone else. Someone like—

"Hey."

—Janet.

No, not someone like Janet. Janet just walked into my office.

"Hey," she says, "what's with Jonah? He looks . . . bad."

"Nothing," I say from behind my hands.

"Did you have a fight?"

"No."

She sits down. I hear the standard-issue chair accept her weight. The rustle of leather as she moves her "piece." You would think my lack of communication would communicate itself, but it doesn't.

"Did you break up?" she asks.

I sigh and move my hands away from eyes. "We didn't have anything to break," I say.

"You didn't . . ." She trails off. "You guys aren't, like, together?"

"We aren't together," I say out loud. For the first time. "We're just friends." The word "friends" hurts. Friends don't hurt each other.

"Oh." She chews on the nail of her right index finger. "So I could ask him to dinner . . . or something?"

Jonah and Janet? The two Js? The fabulous J-dom? I want to reach across my desk and strangle Janet. Kill her now before she has a chance to attach herself to Jonah and suck the life out of him.

The bitch.

"Sure," I say, picking up a pencil to keep my hands occupied. "He'd probably like that."

"What do you think of these earrings?" She swings her head from side to side, making itsy-bitsy tin cows jump over yellow crescent moons.

Making my stomach roll over and play dead.

"Cute," I say. I look down and find my pencil in two pieces. One piece in each hand.

"Do you think Jonah would—?"

"Oh, sure. Sure," I say, still looking at the pencil. It is—was—one of my favorites. "He likes nursery rhymes. All the time. Reading them, I mean. Used to. Grade school. Maybe even preschool, but I didn't know him then."

I'm saved from further inanity by my phone ringing. I pick it up, hoping Janet will leave and let me suffer my guilt monsters alone. She sits there. A bump with a security badge, sitting on a log.

"Hello?"

"What have you done with your sister?" Mom says into my ear.

"Huh?"

"*Give me that,*" I hear Dad say in the background. "*No!*" Mom says. They're tussling for telephone supremacy. They should just get an extension.

I put my hand over the phone and say to Janet, "This will take a while."

She smiles and nods. She sits there. Shifts her gun. A bump with a badge and a firearm, sitting on a log.

"It's a family thing," I say.

She smiles.

"A *private* family thing."

"Oh! I'm sorry." She bounces up off the log. Chair, I mean. "I'll just go find Jonah."

Bitch.

"Is your sister there?" Dad asks. He's breathing a little harder from the effort of getting the phone away from Mom.

"You tell her I don't want my baby hanging around with any of her friends!" Mom says. *"You tell her."*

"She's here," I tell Dad, not bothering to ask the obvious questions. Like how come it took three days for them to notice she was gone?

"Tell her to send that girl home immediately," Mom says.

Apparently, Mom never had any doubts about who was corrupting her baby into running away from home.

"So that's where she is," Dad says. "We thought she was on a class trip."

That explains a few things.

"But she didn't come home with the others," he continues.

"Oh," I say. "Well, she's here."

"Then send her home!"

"Tell her to send her home," Mom says.

"Um . . . I don't think she wants to," I say. "I think she . . . needs a little time—"

"You tell her to get her butt back where it belongs or I'll—"

"You get your butt back in the house, young lady," Dad said.

Framed in the square of light from our kitchen door, I could see Mom peering over his shoulder and out into the yard, where Jonah and I were just finishing the cigarettes he'd brought with him after rocking the green Volvo with Morgan. I hid the cigarette behind my back and tried to drop it and grind it out before Mom or Dad noticed what I was doing. Mom was wearing her pink housedress. The one with calla lilies and a built-in belt.

"See?" Mom said to Dad. "See, I told you this would happen. But you wouldn't believe me. You had to let her—"

"Wichita!" Dad said, not bothering to wait for Mom to finish her "I told you so" monologue. "Move it! Now!"

"See ya," I said to Jonz.

He nodded.

Dad grabbed my shoulder and pushed me into the house, then he walked out to where Jonah still stood. "You little son of a bitch," I heard Dad say. "What the hell do you think you're doing?"

"Just talking," Jonah said.

"No one in your family just talks," Dad said. "They all *do*. You're going to end up just like your father. But fuck me if I'm going to—"

Mom dragged me away before I could hear any more, but not before I saw Jonz reel back from the blow of Dad's words.

I fought to get back outside. I wanted to get in Dad's face. Tell him Jonah wasn't whatever Dad seemed to think he was, but Mom grabbed me.

"You get your butt upstairs where it belongs," she said.

I twisted my arm out of her grasping fingers and reached for the doorknob.

Only the space under the tree was empty.

"You can't do this," I said to Mom. "You can't separate us. He's my friend. And friends don't leave."

She pointed toward the stairs. "Go. Now."

"She'd better get her butt home or else," Dad says.

In bad TV movies, a father's bluster and anger springs forth from the deep, hidden well of caring for his child that will manifest itself openly sometime during the climax of the movie. He'll jump into the fiery inferno or frozen river or simply bail the brat out of jail. Things are simple on TV. Dumbed down for the typical audience of five-year-olds.

Dad is not blustering and ordering because he cares. He's blustering and ordering because his mighty will has been crossed. Mom has nagged him into a frenzy of machismo, and he is exercising his parental authority before his daughter (daughters?) can embarrass him in public. The fact that he does a good job of embarrassing *himself* in public seems to escape him. But maybe the affair with Dolores, Post Office Maiden of Desire, has been going on for so long no one notices anymore.

"I'll talk to her," I say. "Just give her some time."

"Time? She doesn't need time. She needs to get home. Now."

"*She's just a baby,*" Mom says in the background. "*She's not old enough to be gone this long.*"

As much as I'd like to get Geena out of my apartment, the thought of sending her back to Hove and the loving arms of my parents makes me shiver. So I prevaricate—which is a fat thesaurus way to say I lie.

"Let me talk to her," I say again. "We're . . . having a great time, but I'll . . . make sure she gets home."

"You do that," Dad says. Then he hangs up, but not before I hear my mom say, "*Tell her—*"

I press the heels of my hands to my eyes. There's a headache in there and it's dying to come out.

"*You can't do this. You can't separate us. He's my friend. And friends don't leave.*"

I wonder what would happen if the universe opened a black hole and sucked half of the Gemini constellation away. Would the remaining twin wink and go out from loneliness?

Chapter 11

"This will start a 'family situation,'" Jonz said as he reached into the refrigerator. It was a hot summer afternoon in Hove. We were three weeks away from entering high school. Not that it made much difference in a town where all the grades shared a building.

"What will?" I asked, leaning over his shoulder.

He pulled out a paper bag. In black marker his older sister had written on it: CARO'S!!! DON'T TOUCH!

"What is it?" I asked.

He opened the sack. "Oranges. Good thing I like oranges."

"You wouldn't!"

"Caro's been a pain lately." He held the bag up and shook it. "Ready?"

"For what?"

"To create a 'family situation'?"

Giggling, we left the house and walked to the park. I had given Jonz a set of wood-carving tools for his birthday a week ago. Not the big ones. Just the kind that fit in your palm. There was a tree in the park where everyone carved their initials or aging rock and roll symbols or pithy sayings about the mayor's ancestry. It was such an institution you didn't even get in trouble for defacing public property if a cop happened to catch you.

When we reached the tree, I swung up onto one of the lower

branches and dangled my bare, sunburned feet in the air. Jonz closed his eyes until I was settled.

"It's only a few feet up," I said.

He walked over to a nearby merry-go-round and spun it. "It's only going around at twenty-two rpm," he yelled back at me.

I grimaced. "Sorry."

He tossed me an orange. "Get busy pissing off Caro, and I'll forgive the impertinence."

I threw an orange peel at his head.

Family situation.

Something slams into my office window, and I jerk awake. I fell asleep with the heels of my hands pressed into my eyes to keep out the guilt monster, and my vision is blurred from the pressure.

The window.

Getting up, I look out the window. On the ledge, a starling lies on its side, mouth open, eyes closed. It must have flown into the glass and knocked itself out. If it had fallen all the way to the ground . . . I struggle with the swollen window frame. If I can get the bird inside where it's warm, he (she?) might survive the concussion. The window creaks, moans, refuses to budge. I push at it with every last bit of myself I can find.

The window gives in five inches.

Enough.

Ice-cold air wraps around my knees as I kneel down and stretch my hand out for the ledge. Not quite. I push part of my shoulder through, feeling blindly until my fingers close around the feathered bundle. I ease the bird through the crack and settle her into the folds of my scarf.

The window won't shut.

Kenny showed up while I was sleeping. Down in the coffee room, he's practicing for some kind of musical theater audition. I hope the role is "steamboat whistle." He's a natural. And at this rate, Timothy is going to fire him any day now.

"Wichita!" Kenny sings, as I walk into the break room. "Don't leave me, sweet Wichita."

"Can you help me shut my window?" I ask.

The whistling stops. He follows me back to my office. Only the guilt monster has taken on real-life proportions and it's slamming around the room.

I suck in a breath. I'm going to be devoured. But the monster perches on my bookshelf and stares at me.

The starling.

"How'd that bird get in?" Kenny asks.

"She knocked herself out on the window," I say. "I brought her inside."

The starling flies to the window, beats her wings against the glass. Outside, another starling hovers, fluttering just beyond reach. I pick up my scarf. After a few failed attempts, I manage to throw it over the revived bird and ease her out the window. Kenny leans his bulk on the swollen frame, and the window snaps shut.

The starlings are gone.

"Thanks," I say, hanging my scarf over my spare chair. I'm still wearing my coat, and chasing the starling has made me sweat. I start to struggle out of the wool blanket.

"Hey," Kenny says, still leaning on the window, "what's up with Jonah?"

I shrug.

"He quit," Kenny says.

I'm halfway out of my coat, but the world has stopped. "What?"

"Just now. Told Timothy he quit."

"Why?"

"Don't you know?"

I shake my head.

"Neither do I. Keep the window shut, now." He straightens up and walks out of my office.

"Where's Timothy?" I ask, but Kenny's already in full-throat cry. Something about the show going on.

The world stops being stopped. The room tilts and slowly begins to turn around. A giant office merry-go-round. I drop my coat onto the floor and make it to the bathroom just in time to lose my empty stomach in the toilet.

I'm rinsing my mouth at the sink when Dorothy steps out of the other stall. She's as white as I am.

"Ooo," she moans. "After the twins, I swore I wasn't going to do this again." She hands me a paper towel. "When are you due?"

"I'm not," I say. But she's not listening.

"Just make sure the baby isn't early or you'll end up in the coffee room. God, that was embarrassing."

"Yeah." I leave before she can say anything else.

I run into Timothy just outside the door. "You," he says. Then he leans in close to my face. "What's with you?"

"I'm sick," I say. A goddamn lie, but I look the part. White, clammy, shaking.

"I don't care if you're sick," Timothy says. "What the hell did you do to Jonah? I'm never going to find another person with his eye. Do you think I can hire someone with his expertise by putting an ad in the fucking paper?"

I stare at him.

"If I could afford a bigger headache, I'd fire *you* right now because *I* am really *pissed*," Timothy continues, stabbing a finger at me. "We've got that weaving exhibit coming in tomorrow and I *need* Jonah to—" He breaks off and throws his hands into the air.

The museum is sort of a home away from home, if you know what I mean. We're a kind of pseudofamily. Usually a happy pseudofamily. Just not today. So while some people might find what Timothy is saying a little off, it's perfectly normal around here.

"What—?"

"What's with you two?" Timothy asks, cutting me off. "Can't you keep your little lovers' spats out of the office?"

"We're not lovers," I say.

"It's unprofessional," he continues, ignoring me.

"It wasn't a lovers' spat."

"And now I have to set up the whole goddamn exhibit myself. If I didn't *need* you, I'd fire *you*."

"So *fire* me," I say, sounding more like Kenny the human steam whistle than myself.

"No," Timothy yells back. "I should make *you* put up the exhibit."

"I'm not an art historian."

"That's right," he says. "You're the reason I don't *have* an art historian."

"I didn't do *anything!*" I say, knowing it's a lie and not caring.

"I *ought* to fire you."

"Do it!"

"No!"

"I'll set up the exhibit," Jonz says from behind me.

I turn around fast enough to get nauseated again. Jonah looks clammy and pale. Like he's been throwing up in the men's bathroom down the hall.

We stare at each other.

One long, long, long moment.

Separated.

He breaks the stare and looks at Timothy.

"I'll set it up," he says again, then he walks past us and down the hall to his office.

"Well, then. Okay," Timothy says. I can feel him looking at me, but I'm watching Jonah's back. "If you're sick," Timothy says to me, "leave." Then he walks past me and up the hall in the opposite direction.

Jonah goes into his office without looking back at me.

I slam a fist into the very solid, very hard, cement and cinder block wall.

"Take it easy," Janet says as she walks by with a cup of coffee. "What the heck is your problem, anyway?"

I don't answer. I'm too busy leaning over and cradling my injured hand.

I stood by the big oak in our front yard, bent over and gasping as I cradled my hand to my chest.

"Leave me alone," I said to Jonah when I heard him come up behind me.

He didn't leave.

I rubbed my hand. It wasn't fair that the anger hurt so bad I had to hit something, only to hurt myself worse.

Mom had found us making cocoa. "You're making a mess of my kitchen," she'd said. "Can't you do anything right?"

"It's just cocoa," I'd said, not thinking about what I was saying, not remembering that Mom had been up with a cranky toddler all last night and most of the day.

"And you're making it in my kitchen," she'd said. "And it's after five. What are you doing with chocolate after five? No caffeine after five."

"It's cocoa," I'd said again, but Mom was already dumping it down the drain.

"Out," she'd said. "Get out." Then she'd thrown the pot across the kitchen, dark drops of cocoa streaming in the pot's wake.

I'd slammed out and gone to the tree.

"Try a flat surface next time," Jonz said, sliding down to sit with his back to the tree. "Tree bark's a bitch."

I looked down at him.

"Shaking your hand helps." He demonstrated, flapping his fingers like a distraught European.

I tried it and some of the ache left, but the air moving over my cut knuckles stung. After a few more shakes, I sat down beside him. Red embarrassment crept over me. I wasn't any better than my mother. There's not much difference between throwing a pot and throwing a punch.

"I'm sorry," I said, digging a bare toe into the dirt. "About the cocoa and about . . ." I waved my swelling hand.

He caught my hand and rubbed the fingers. "It's okay."

I pulled my hand away as soon as I could without looking like a baby.

I shake my hand, trying to get rid of the ache. Cement is a flat surface, but flat surfaces aren't much better than tree bark.

Dorothy peers out from around the bathroom door. She sees me and shuts the door again.

"It's okay," I say. "I'm leaving."

"Hormones," she says through the closed door. "Being pregnant does a number on your hormones."

"I'm not pregnant," I say as I walk up the hall to my office.

Hormones aren't my problem. My problem is genes.

I sit down behind my desk. Suck my bleeding knuckle. My hand throbs. My coat rings.

I stare at it. Ignore it. The ringing stops, then starts up again. And again.

"Geena's gone," Dylan says before I can say hello.

"What do you mean she's gone?" I ask.

He sniffs. "All her things are gone. I went out . . . she told me to get some doughnuts. I don't know where she got the money—"

I picture my Eiffel Tower piggy bank on the dresser. The one with my laundry quarters in it.

"—but she gave me a bunch of change and sent me out. When I got back . . ." He moans slightly, and I can practically see him grabbing his hair and leaning his elbows on his knees.

Only that's Jonah. This is Dylan.

"Right," I say, banishing the Jonah image. "Is the car there?"

"Hold on. I'll check."

My hand is bleeding again. I put my knuckle back into my mouth. My blood tastes like salty guilt.

"It's here," he says.

A vague part of me was hoping Geena might have packed her bags and run home to Mommy and Daddy after living two days with her evil sister.

Guess not.

"I'll be there as soon as I can," I tell Dylan. "Just stay put." The last thing I need is *two* lost souls on my hands.

I run into Timothy in the hall. "I've got a . . . family situation," I say.

He shrugs. "What else is new?"

Did I ever mention that Timothy can get real petty when his panties are in a wad? It happens.

"I'm serious," I say.

"So am I," he says. "Jonah is leaving after this exhibit, and now you want an extended vacation, right? What about me? What about my needs?"

Guilt twists a little in my back. "Look," I say, "I'll talk to Jonah, okay?"

He shrugs. "Whatever. Pack your things and leave if you want."

Okay, so the museum can be a bit like a *dysfunctional* pseudofamily. That's us. Just one great, big, happy, dysfunctional family. Whee.

I put on my coat, grab my bag, and walk down to Jonah's office. He's not there. I finally find him in the south exhibit room.

"You shouldn't have to leave," I say after five minutes of waiting for him to notice me. I gesture toward the room, even though he isn't looking at me and can't see the gesture. "You shouldn't have to leave here just because of me."

"Who says I'm leaving because of you?" he asks. He makes a note on the clipboard in his hand.

I'm not sure what to say. "No one."

"Maybe I stayed here because of you," he says. "And now I can leave."

He's got his back to me, deliberately not looking at me. Normally, this wouldn't be a problem, but right now it pisses me off. "I thought you liked it here."

"Maybe I did." He turns around and smiles at me. A very un-Jonah-like smile. Or at least it's not the kind of smile Jonah gives *me.*

"I'm leaving," I say, not knowing that I was leaving until this moment. "No need for both of us to go."

"Really? Where to?"

I open my mouth to tell him about Geena, then I shut it. I wanted free of the flock, didn't I? The individual takes care of her problems . . . individually. Geminus alone.

"Nowhere," I say out loud. "Maybe *I* stayed here because of *you.*"

He laughs.

"So you can stay put," I say. "It's all yours. You don't have to quit."

"You know," he says, setting pedestals on either side of the door to the exhibit room, "for someone who doesn't know how to talk, you have a lot to say about how other people should do things."

I stare at him, but he's eyeballing the alignment of the pedestals flanking the door.

"Fuck you," I say. And I leave.

"Ow," Jonah said, rubbing his arm in mock agony as we lay on the grass of the football field and looked at the stars. "What'd you hit me for?"

"Because it was a dumb horoscope," I said.

"You don't think we'll be friends forever?" he asked.

"Of course we will," I said. "That's why it was so dumb. Anyone would know that."

"So it's only dumb if it's true?"

I wanted to hit him again.

A star shot across the sky, leaving a trail of reddish afterglow in its wake.

"Make a wish," Jonah said.

Friends forever, I thought, watching the afterglow disappear. Just in case. Just in case.

"Fuck you," I say. And I leave.

Outside the museum, it's snowing. The flakes leave a red afterglow when they fall past tears.

Chapter 12

Life needs a pause button. Something to make it so you can catch your breath and just *think* for a minute or two. Maybe I should ask God about this. After all, he gave me a new name, didn't he?

I stumble up the stairs to my apartment and try to think around the mess in my head. Hunting for one sixteen-year-old pregnant girl who wants to be lost in Chicago is comparable to hunting for the proverbial needle in the haystack. There's no point in panicking and running through the streets grabbing every red-haired, freckled girl and twirling her around to see if she's Geena. It's not surprising that I catch Dylan on his way out of my apartment to do just that.

"I told you to stay put," I say, shooing him back through the door.

"She's out there all by herself—" he begins.

"—because she wants to be," I finish for him.

This sounds callous, and he gives me another one of those "you'd give her a box and show her the alley" looks I'm beginning to hate.

"I did *not* throw her out," I say.

"As good as."

I toss my bag onto the couch and take off my coat. "Because I told her she needed to get a job?"

He throws himself onto the couch beside my bag and scowls at me. "Because you told your parents you'd take her back home."

Insert screechy, time-halt sound effect here.

"Whoa, whoa, whoa. Hold on a minute. I told my parents *what?*"

"That you'd take her back." He folds his arms over his chest Bruce Lee–style, pushing his tattooed biceps out with his hands. I stare at a twisting dragon. The dragon winks at me.

"I never—" I start to say, then break off.

Did I? Everything was so confused. . . . I think back to the phone call and listen to myself say something about talking to Geena, but did I . . . ?

No. I didn't.

"I never said anything about making Geena go back to Hove. Did they call here?"

He nods. "Just before lunch."

I want to throttle my parents. No, I want to throttle Geena for believing them. But what could I expect? I left home when Geena was five. She has no way of knowing I'm not going to drive her back to the loving arms of the two people who inhabit the house of her birth. Okay, so she was born in Hove General, but you know what I mean. She doesn't know me. What could I expect?

I could expect her to act with a bare modicum of self-preservation. And it is not in the interest of preserving one's self that one packs one's bags and leaves to wander the streets of Chicago the first week of March. In like a lion and all that.

Dylan is making a second escape attempt.

"What are you going to do?" I ask. "Wander the streets and hope you'll run into her during the five minutes you aren't lost?"

Dylan's a nice boy, but I'm having a really bad day.

Okay, so it's my fault I'm having a bad day. But other people are helping to make it worse. And it looks pretty stupid to try and kick your own butt, so it's easier to kick someone else's.

"I'm sorry," I say to Dylan as he sulks back to the couch. "Try and work with me, all right? There's a pen in the outer pocket of my bag. The first thing to do is figure out where all Geena could have gone with . . ." I stop to think. How many quarters did I have in that piggy bank? Not many. I did laundry last weekend. "How much money did Geena give you this morning?"

"About ten bucks."

"Ten?" I could have sworn there was no more than five. . . .

A really nasty realization comes to my cloudy brain. I open the door to India's room and, yes, we have a serious problem on our hands.

India's ceramic Maneki Neko cat—the one rubbing his left ear for good luck—is lying in bits and pieces on top of her dresser.

India's Maneki Neko cat *bank*—the one with all those bits and pieces India's been saving for the last nine months since she moved in with me—just saw its ninth life hammered to dust and all its monetary guts ripped out.

My sister is a thief.

I am in big trouble.

"You're in big trouble, young lady!"

Mom's voice. She had just pulled the car up beside me. I was so happy to see her, I didn't notice what she was saying. Somehow, I hadn't been able to find my way home. Everything was so different and I didn't recognize any of the houses. Even the train tracks seemed to be going in the wrong direction.

"Where have you been?" she said as I climbed into the Impala and tried to pull the heavy door shut using both of my six-year-old arms. I finally got the door to close.

"I went to see a dog," I said. And just thinking about it made me forget how scared I'd been walking between all those strange houses next to the weeds and bottles along the tracks.

After school, after the humiliating experience of puking all over him, Jonah had remembered his promise and he'd taken me to see his dog. Shep was a really nice dog. Black and white and hairy, and he licked your face if you let him.

"Can we get a dog?" I asked.

"Whose dog? Where did you go?" Mom asked instead of answering.

"Jonah's." For the first time I noticed that Mom's face was red, and that her hair hung in sweaty stripes on her neck. "He's in my class," I added, because I'd learned that sometimes if you added more details it meant you wouldn't get yelled at.

"You didn't come home after school because you went to see a god-damn *dog?*" The Impala's engine made an unhappy sound as Mom turned the key in the ignition with the car already running.

"I'm sorry," I whispered, pulling myself into the corner made by the seat and the door.

She put the car into drive, then slammed it back into park. "Jonah? Jonah *LiaKos?* You've been over at the LiaKoses' house?"

"N-no." I tried to remember. Did Jonah have a last name? "I don't know," I said, adding what information I could.

"God-*damn* it!" Mom hit the steering wheel with the palm of her hand. Then she hit it again.

I pushed myself farther into the corner, but she grabbed my arm and pulled me out of what I'd begun to consider safety.

"Don't you *ever*," she said, hot and in my face, "don't you *ever* go and see that dog again."

Then she pulled me between her breasts and the steering wheel and spanked me until I cried.

I am in big trouble.

My sister is a thief.

And she's too big to spank. Although I'm not sure that will stop me.

Dylan comes up behind me and looks into India's room. "What?" he asks. Then he sees the poor ceramic kitty. "Uh . . . Wichita? Do you think—?"

"What do *you* think?" I interrupt, all nasty and bitchy. Then I let out a long breath. It's not Dylan's fault. He's just along for the ride.

No. That didn't sound quite right.

An (only slightly) hysterical burble of noise breaks free of my throat. Dylan stares at me.

"I have to call India," I say, "and find out how much she had." I'm hoping it's in the tens and not the hundreds or—God forbid—the thousands. I'll never be able to repay—

Wait a minute! Why should I repay anything? Righteous anger makes my spine stiff until I realize that if India is going to be appeased, it will be me that pays her back and not Geena the shiftless thief.

You just left your job, a naughty voice whispers in my head.

Oh, shut up, I tell it.

I dial India's cell number and get an out-of-range response. I leave a message with the receptionist at the printing press where India works, but I don't expect the distraught woman—who was trying to answer three lines and eat a sandwich all at once—to actually pass the message on to India within the next thirty-six hours.

I sit down opposite Dylan and hand him a piece of paper to go with the pen from my bag. "You know her best," I tell him, "so this part is up to you. Where do you think she would go?"

He gives me a helpless look. "I don't know," he says. "In Hove, she'd be at the Burger King or out by the lake, but I don't know anything about Chicago."

"Neither does she."

He gets that "head out the door to get lost" look on his face again.

"Take a deep breath," I say. "I meant that she doesn't have some secret well of knowledge you don't have. Just write down all the things she likes to do and places she might go."

He starts writing. I'm trying to figure out how far she'd get in a taxi if I assume that India's kitty didn't hold more than fifty.

Not far if she gets a taxi driver who graduated from the eight-step program and whose meter isn't working. I have a vague image of Geena flopping into the back seat and asking how far fifty bucks will get her. *"About a block,"* says the driver, all his teeth involved in Step #6: the winning smile.

The image doesn't help.

When Dylan hands me his list, I'm hoping Geena isn't quite *that* stupid. I read it out loud. "Pizza Hut, Burger King, the mall . . . Sleepy Eye Inn?" I look up at him and he ducks and blushes. "They rented you a room?"

He nods, still blushing.

"Man, things have really *changed* in Hove," I say. "Whatever happened to the Moral Majority?" I don't exactly expect an answer, so I keep reading the list. "Martha's place—"

"I just wrote down everywhere I could think of," he interrupts. "Those are all in Hove."

I already had that figured out.

I mentally add Dylan to Santa's Naughty Boys with Dense Brains list.

My cell rings. It's India. "I've got bad news," I say, and I tell her about Geena's absconding with Maneki Neko's guts.

India is quiet. Too quiet.

"I'll pay back every penny," I tell her. "I'll buy you a new kitty. It's all a big misunderstanding. She thought—"

"It's okay," India says. "I have a little sister, too. You wouldn't like her."

"I don't like little sisters, period. At least not today," I add, catching a morose look from Dylan. "Do you know how much was in there?"

"I'm not sure." In my mind, I can see India shrug her feline shrug. "Seventy-five? A hundred, maybe. I haven't counted it in a while."

And I was hoping for fifty or less. Dang.

"Look," India says, "things are slow here today. I could come back and help you look for her if you want."

I love this woman. She's a damn good liar, too, because I can hear a lot of yelling in the background and it sounds anything but slow over there today.

"Thanks," I tell her. "Just stay put. Dylan and I are about to head out the door."

Dylan gives me a perky schoolgirl smile.

Chapter 13

About five minutes after Jonah and I arrived in Chicago, the rusty wreck that had cost me half my Burger King savings collapsed. I never replaced it. Walking is good for you, and friends with vehicles are usually accommodating if there's a heart attack or a job interview on a day when it's pouring rain—days when CTA just won't take care of you. Today is the first time I've wasted a wishful thought on the rusty wreck since I saw it being pulled out of my life by the tow truck. I'm thinking about it because Dylan and I are on foot and walking in circles.

Walking in circles is usually an idea linked with being lost or doing something utterly useless. We're not lost, but I have to admit that our efforts pretty much fall into the utterly useless category. We're actually walking in ever larger circles, using my apartment as the center.

"We should split up," Dylan says for the Nth time.

I patiently explain how much I look forward to searching for *two* lost people. For the Nth time.

"Geena's not lost," he says. "She's never lost."

I patiently ask why she called me from Joliet if she never gets lost.

Dylan goes quiet and tucks his chin into his scarf. The movement reminds me of Jonah, and a nasty little animal claws its way into my chest.

I read a book once where this guy got into a motorcycle wreck or a Ferrari wreck or something and had to have his crushed foot amputated.

At night he would wake up, and the bottom of his missing foot itched. Itched even though the foot was in some hospital dump or incinerator or whatever they do with discarded body parts that aren't worth anything.

The foot was cut off, but it was still there in his mind.

How long will Jonah still be in my mind?

More utterly useless circling. I've done the deed. And just like every decision and action and amputation, I'm going to have worries about possible regrets and possible failures. The trick is to ignore the worries. Works every time.

"What's up?" Jonah asked when he slid open his window.

I shrugged.

"Hang on." He shut the window. A few minutes later, he slipped out the front door and walked over to where I stood waiting. "You shouldn't come around here at night," he said.

I tossed the rocks I was still holding in my hand out onto the ground. "This is Hove," I said. "Nothing's going to happen." Twelve and full of myself.

Jonz frowned and glanced back at the house, but he didn't say anything. Something fell over inside, and I could hear a woman laughing.

"Mom's having a baby," I said.

"Yeah?"

"She says it's my fault."

We started walking down toward the railroad tracks. Far away across the grass and hollows, a train whistle wailed. Reaching our ears by riding on the humid night air.

"Why?" Jonz asked as we scuffed along the gravel of the rail bed.

"Because she was trying to keep Dad around." I kicked what I thought was an empty beer can and managed to stub my toe, as the can rolled away dribbling dark liquid onto the gravel.

"That's not your fault," he said, waiting for me to rub feeling back into my stinging toe. I hated wearing shoes and snuck out barefoot whenever I could.

"I know. But try telling that to Mom."

"She's just worried."

"No, she's not," I said, starting to walk again. "She's just sorry."

"Maybe she was trying to do something right and it turned out all wrong."

Anger hit my stomach. Mom blamed me because she was going to be all fat, waddly, and pregnant. What was so hard to get about that? "Why are you taking her side?" I asked.

He stopped. "I'm not. You can't do anything about it. About her having a baby, I mean. So there's no point getting all worked up about something she said, right?"

I glared at him. "That's not the point."

"Yeah?" He dug the heel of his shoe into the gravel. We were standing next to the railroad crossing. The silent crossing. I screamed when the bar came down across the road and the lights and bells started flashing. "You can't worry about everything," Jonz said.

And he walked out into the middle of the tracks.

My mouth hung open. Over the sound of the flashing light and bell I could hear the click-clack of the train.

"Don't be an idiot," I yelled.

"The trick is to ignore the stuff you don't like," Jonz said. "Stuff you're worried about."

"Get off the tracks." He ignored me, so I slipped under the bar and grabbed his arm. "Come *on!*"

He pulled back. Stronger. Able to stay right where he wanted to be.

"Jonah," I begged. "Please."

But no one could hear me over the sound of the train. Especially if the person I wanted to hear me had his eyes closed and his arms stretched out over the tracks. Jesus on the cross waiting to be hit in the face by a million tons of moving steel.

I grabbed his outstretched hand and I pulled. Hard. Laughing, he let himself come my way. Falling into me just as the train whipped into the crossing.

"Are you worried still?" he asked.

"You son of a *bitch*," I screamed over the click-clacks of the spinning wheels.

"Works every time," he said.

The trick is to ignore the worries. Works every time. And ignorance is a lot less costly than playing chicken with a diesel engine.

Dylan and I are standing in front of a KFC. We've seen it before. It's the conclusion of our latest circle. The tail of the snake in the snake's mouth. My cell rings.

"I need help," Geena says in my ear.

"Where the hell are you?" I ask.

"I got picked up," Geena says. "Can you bail me out?"

Dylan is grabbing for the phone. I turn around so my body blocks his attempts. Shades of Mom and Dad. "Where are you?"

"The cops," Geena says. "The cops picked me up. They thought I was . . . trying to pick up this guy."

"Where are you?" I ask again.

Geena answers a question someone on the other side is asking, then: "The cops picked me up," she says again, and I swear she's crying. My tough-as-nails, sixteen and pregnant, thieving little sister is crying.

I ease my voice down a notch. "It's okay," I tell her. "I'll come and get you. But I need to know where you are."

"I don't *know*," she wails.

Closing my eyes, I take a deep breath for patience and fend off another phone-abduction attempt by Dylan. "How far did you go after you left?" I ask, trying a different method.

"I don't know. A few miles?"

"Okay," I say. "I think I know where you are. I'll—we'll—be there as soon as we can." Then I hand the phone to Dylan.

As the two young lovers ease each other's pain, I realize that I'm glad this worry is over.

"Works every time," Jonz said. We were holding on to each other's arms and the train was screaming past us and we were screaming and laughing and I didn't care anymore about Mom blaming me for anything because we were both alive with blood pounding in our veins.

"Hey! What are you kids doing?"

We turned into the spotlight the cop had trained on us. An oncoming headlamp. We started laughing again.

The cop climbed out of his car, throwing shadows on us as he tucked his billy club into his belt while walking between us and the spot. He shone a flashlight into Jonah's face. "Huh. Another LiaKos. Trying to end your life early? It'd probably be a good thing."

Jonah's smile dipped in tune to the dip in my chest.

The cop flicked the flashlight beam over and into my eyes. "Who are you?"

"He was just walking me home," I said. "We weren't doing anything." Trying to give extra information so we wouldn't get yelled at.

"How nice. And where exactly is your home?"

I gave him the address.

"Well, get in the car and I'll take you there. You," he shines the light back at Jonah, "you get your sorry ass back indoors before I bust you for breaking curfew."

I think I forgot to mention that Hove is one of those . . . annoying towns where every kid under eighteen is locked up after nine P.M. They have to keep you off the streets, you know. You might do something wicked at nine oh one.

Of course, they have to catch you first in order to lock you up.

I climbed into the back seat of the squad car and watched Jonah get smaller as we went in opposite directions.

"You ought to be happy I didn't haul you both in," the cop said into his rearview mirror.

"She's lucky I didn't drop her in the tank," Officer O'Reilly says to me after I finally locate the right station. "But she says it was all a misunderstanding." He doesn't believe that for a second. He was moved by Geena's way with tears. Just like Dylan, who's holding my sister while she sobs into his shoulder.

"She got picked up for soliciting," O'Reilly continues.

I'm picturing someone handing out illegal handbills. Then I get what he means. Remember what Geena said on the phone. Oh. *That* kind of soliciting. Duh. I raise my eyebrows at Geena.

She breaks off her tears long enough to say, "I wasn't. I wasn't." But her gaze slides over to some point above my left shoulder.

Uh-huh.

"I was just asking for directions," Geena says.

Sure she was.

"It's okay," I say out loud. "Just a misunderstanding."

"I should call SRS," O'Reilly says. It takes me a minute to figure out he's talking to me.

"SRS?"

"She's sixteen. Wandering around the streets with all her bags?" He gives me a "you're a bad little mommy" look.

"I'm her sister," I say.

The cop blushes. "Oh."

"She's . . . visiting," I say. "I told you about the laundry room in my building, didn't I?" I say to Geena. "You didn't need to haul all your clothes somewhere else." For three scary seconds I'm not sure she'll catch on, but she does.

She sniffs. "No, you didn't. I was asking that . . . that *awful* man where I could find a Laundromat, but he thought I was . . ." She bats her eyelashes at the cop. "He thought I was trying to do something . . . naughty."

The eyelashes might be a bit much.

I hold my breath, but O'Reilly either falls for it or decides to fall for it. "I'm sorry about all this," he says to me, to Geena, to Dylan, who's patting Geena's shoulder and looking about as protective as a seventeen-year-old boy can look. Which isn't a whole heck of a lot when he's confused and scared. "Just a misunderstanding," O'Reilly continues. "You might as well take her home."

Just a misunderstanding.

"Here you are," the cop said as he pulled up in front of my house. I tried to get out, but the door wouldn't open. The cop took his time walking around to let me out. Then he put a cold hand on the back of my neck and walked me up the sidewalk, where he knocked on our door, dislodging the grapevine wreath with the silk pansies.

Dad opened the door. He looked from the cop to me. "Wichita? Why aren't you upstairs in your room?"

I pushed my toe against the bare arch of my other foot. "I—" I began, but the cop interrupted me. I heard the name LiaKos. The word "train." Mom appeared behind Dad. Her hair was down, hanging around her face and over her shoulders. The cop stopped talking as Mom grabbed me and dragged me through the door and into the kitchen.

"Where have you been?" she asked. "What did you do?"

"Nothing," I said.

"You've been out with that boy. You little slut."

Then she slapped me.

She had never hit me. Okay, I'd been spanked, but she'd never hit me in the face. We stared at each other. My cheek burned in the heat of the kitchen. Mom's hair foamed around her neck.

Dad walked in just as Mom grabbed my shoulders. "You are never going to see that boy again if—"

"It was just a misunderstanding, Maggie," Dad said. "Leave her alone."

I looked up at him, grateful for support in the face of Mom's fury, only he wasn't supporting me. He was digging at Mom.

Mom froze in midshake. Tears formed in the inner corners of her eyes and her lip trembled. She slapped me again. Then she slapped Dad. "Fuck you, Brad," she said, before walking out of the kitchen.

The second slap didn't leave a mark, but it hurt even more because of those tears.

Whistling, Dad grabbed a can of caffeinated Coke and went back to watching the game.

Just a misunderstanding.

"It was just a big misunderstanding," Geena says. She's sitting on the couch, all pout and trembling lips.

I sit down across from her. "Dylan, would you mind making some coffee?" I ask. I don't think he knows how, but he seems eager to try.

"Cut it out with the lip," I say to Geena. The lip stops trembling. Oddly enough, I don't feel angry. I feel tired. Too tired to make sense. But

I try. I try to form sentences in my head, but throw each one away before I can give it voice.

"So when did you decide to become a pregnant teen hooker?" I ask after all the other questions have been discarded. The words come out natural and conversational, as if I were talking to a stranger's child at a party. *"So why do you want to be a fireman, Johnny?"*

"A what?" Her eyes widen until she looks like a cat. A Maneki Neko cat, for that matter. "I was just asking for directions. I told you."

"No, that's what you told Mr. Bewildered Police Officer."

"You don't *believe* me!" Her eyes get wider—if that's possible—and the lip starts to come out again. Then, as if she's finally figured out I'm on to the lip trick, she shoves her shoulders back into the couch and crosses her arms across her chest. "You don't believe me."

"It's kind of hard to believe my own lie," I tell her.

She squeezes her chest a little harder and stares at the coffee table. I hope she's reading the future in its glass top, but I doubt it. "It wasn't a lie," she says. Nope, she's not reading the future.

"Come on, Geena," I say, starting to feel some anger through the exhaustion. "I made up the story about the Laundromat."

"Yeah? Well, it was true. The asking directions part, I mean." She looks up at me through her eyelashes. She's obviously used to working with Dad. Dad always fell for the Lauren Bacall eyelash thing. "Why don't you believe me?"

"Maybe because you stole seventy-five bucks from my roommate and smashed her cat," I say.

I can see the presses rolling in her brain, working to print out a new excuse, a new lie. "I only took about . . ." Her gaze slides over my shoulder again. "I only took twenty dollars."

"Seventy-five."

She chews the tip of her finger. "Maybe it was. I don't remember."

"Jesus, Geena," I say. Frustration is gaining on exhaustion. The hare catching up with the tortoise.

"You don't understand," she says. "I had to get away." She shifts her weight. "Are we done? 'Cuz I gotta pee."

That's when I lose it.

Chapter 14

I'm not a fan of hysterical behavior. Sometimes when I go to the grocery store, I run into a red-faced child who's got a death grip on the candy display and is attempting to shout down the parental walls of Jericho. I tend to cringe and make tracks for a vacant aisle, even if the aisle contains nothing but Hamburger Helper and canned anchovies. I don't go to sports bars for the same reason. The last time I tried out a sports bar, some guy (child?) threw a mug through the forty-inch television screen when the poor bastard on the football team missed a field goal. Pandemonium ensued.

When I left home, I thought I was done with hysteria. I haven't dropped to the floor, smashed my fist into anything, or done any of my genetic behaviors since . . . well, at least six or nine months.

I've lost it twice today.

At Jonah.

At my sister.

Yelling. Screaming like an out-of-control stranger.

Stranger? Ha.

Screaming like my mother.

Geena stares up at me. Her mouth is hanging open. I realize I'm standing over her like some avenging Valkyrie. Wait. That's wrong.

Valkyries carry brave warriors off the battlefield and up to Val—
Val-something. Paradise. Heaven. I have no intention of carrying my
sister to paradise. Maybe I'm just one of those hovering ravens, waiting
for carrion.

No, not a raven. Worse.

"I want to go home," Geena says. And then she covers her face with
her hands and sobs.

Dylan rushes in where even fools would fear to tread. "Take it easy,"
he says to me. "You're making her feel bad." He sits down beside Geena
and tries to pry her hands away from her face.

Embarrassment and residual anger make me snotty. "Good. I didn't
know it was possible."

"I wanna go *home*," she says through her fingers.

She's saved by the sound of the phone ringing. Because I have an
entire Bible's worth of things to say about people who run away from
home, steal their sister's roommate's money, turn tricks on the nearest
street corner, lie about it, then want to run back home again.

Maybe I'm the one saved by the phone. My guess is that the scripture
reading would have turned into a Bible's worth of screeching. And we've
had quite enough of *that*.

We have, but Mom hasn't.

"Is she there?" Mom says into my ear when I pick up the phone. Even
given the tinny sound on the phone lines between here and Hove, I'd have
to say that Mom's voice is stretched to a high, thin sound. "Is Geena
there?"

I almost run interference and say that Geena's out hunting for some
Chicago flavor, but I give in to a petty desire to get even. "Here," I say to
Geena, and I hand her the phone. "It's for you."

The high-pitched whine from the phone is audible halfway across the
room. Dylan gives me another "box in the alley" look.

"I'm not throwing her out," I tell him. "She deserves it, but I'm not going to do it, okay?"

He frowns at me. "I thought you'd be different," he says. I'm not sure what he means, but he clarifies it for me before he goes back into the kitchen. "I thought you'd be nice to her."

The cliche goes like this: "I hope you'll have a kid just like you someday." I've never actually heard a mother say that in real life, but I see it a lot on TV and read it in the comics. Usually with the joke that the kid gets to look up at his or her parent and say, "Grandma says I'm just like you were when you were my age." And the whole complicated cliche helps enforce the idea that no matter how hard you try, you can't change things. *Plus ça change, plus c'est la même chose.* The more things change, the more they stay the same. That sort of thing. Don't even bother to try. You'll just make the same mistakes.

Since I wasn't allowed to go see Jonah's dog anymore, I made the six-year-old decision that we could spend time at my house instead. Jonz—I didn't call him Jonz yet, actually—Jonah looked as lost as I'd felt when I'd been walking home from his house, but he tried not to show it.

I'd never brought anyone home before, so I thought I'd have to do something special. Special meant cookies. We had eaten about half a bag of Oreos with milk when Mom came through the door, a sack of groceries under each arm.

She stared at us.

We stared at her.

Lines formed around her mouth, and I began to wonder if maybe milk and cookies wasn't the approved method of entertaining.

"This is Jonah, Mom," I said. "That's my mom," I said to Jonah.

He nodded. "Nice to meet you."

It sounded so adult. I was proud.

Mom dropped the groceries onto the counter. "Go home," she said. And her voice sounded the same as when she shooed a stray dog out of the flower bed. "Go on. Go."

"Mom!"

Jonah slid out of the chair. "I'll see you, Cheetah," he said.

After the screen door slammed behind him, Mom turned to me. "I thought I told you—" she began.

"I thought you would be nice to him," I cried. I pushed away from the table and ran upstairs. I saw my glass of milk fall onto the floor, but I didn't care.

"I thought you'd be nice to her."

So. I guess it's possible for cliches to come true. In a way. It's not really fair because I opted to bypass mommyhood, so shouldn't I be exempt? Can't I opt out of this particular cycle of being?

Next thing you know, I'll find out that the sky is a blanket with holes and the rapture was yesterday.

Geena hands me the phone. In a sort of antonym of Mom and Dad's fight for the phone, I put my hands behind my back and try to refuse the thing emitting demonic howls. Geena holds it up in front of my face . . .

. . . and drops it.

Reflex, and the threat of losing a forty-dollar phone, has me catching it. I glare at her.

She glares back.

I hold the phone about six inches from my ear and yell, "Mom, it's Wichita. Take a deep breath before you pass out."

The howling stops.

I risk putting the phone to my ear. "It's okay," I tell her. "We're all fine. Just finished eating a pizza."

Suspicious silence. "Geena said you were having fried chicken."

"Um . . . buffalo wings. You can get them delivered with your pizza."

"Bring that child home. You'll stunt her growth feeding her crap like that."

I sit down in my chair, wrap my free arm around my knees, and rock back and forth to keep from laughing. The child is having a child, so whose growth should we be worried about? "You want me to send them— *her* home?"

"I want you to *bring* her home. And that boy she's usually with. I'm sure he's there, too. You can't hide that from *me*."

Right.

"I have a job, Mom."

"No, you don't."

"What?"

"I called the museum. Someone named Janet said that you'd quit."

Shit. If I ever catch Janet without her firearm, I'm gonna . . .

"It's not official yet," I say, hedging.

"You have to drive them home," she says. "That *boy* doesn't have a license. Neither does your sister."

I rock harder.

"I'll think about it," I say.

"You'll *do* it."

"You'll *do* it," Mom said. "You'll stay away from that boy."

"He's my *friend!*" I said. If I'd thought dropping to the floor and scream-ing would work, I would have tried it. Why did adults always think they could tell other people what to do?

"The happy sounds of home," Dad said, as he banged through the screen door. Mom and I had been so caught up in our . . . discussion, we hadn't heard the car. It was already dark, and if I'd been capable of thinking about anything but Mom driving Jonah away from the table like a stray dog and how unfair life was, I might have wondered why supper was cold.

"Nice of you to drop in, Brad," Mom said. "Maybe it's time Daddy dealt with a few things."

"Daddy, huh?" Dad said, hunting through the fridge for a beer. "What'd you do?" he asks me.

"I want Jonah to be my friend," I said.

Dad popped the tab on the beer can. "Sounds fine to me," he said, shrugging. "I'm going to watch the game."

Mom grabbed his arm. "You can't—"

"What's the matter, Maggie?" Dad asked, looking down at her hand. "You afraid she'll turn out just like you?"

She let go of his arm.

Silence.

I could hear the football game start up in the living room. I waited, not sure what to expect.

"Mom?" I asked after what seemed like an eternity. "Can I—?"

"Just do what you want," Mom said. And she sounded tired.

"Just do whatever you want," I say.

"I want to go home," Geena says.

We're sitting at the table and I'm pretending to drink the coffee Dylan made. I never thought I'd meet someone capable of making coffee that tastes worse than mine.

"Is it okay?" Dylan asks, pointing to the coffee. "I wasn't sure—"

"It's great," I tell him. "Thank you." And I try to smile and chew coffee at the same time.

"Did you hear me?" Geena asks.

"I heard you," I say. "The problem is, I don't *want* to take you back to Hove."

She folds her arms. "I want to go home."

"Then why'd you leave it?"

She scowls. "You don't know what they're like."

"Of course not. I only lived with them for seventeen years."

The sarcasm sails over her head. "At least they're nice to me. Not like you."

"Of course they are," I say. "They're posing for the Loving Parents of the Year poster next week. Let's remember to get together in twenty years and reminisce about our happy childhoods."

"You're such a bitch," Geena says.

"Takes one to know one," I say. Very adultlike, of course.

"Hey!" Dylan says. And I realize he's been trying to get our attention for a while, but we were too busy going at each other to notice.

"Look," he says, when we both turn to look at him, "can you guys just stop fighting for five minutes?"

Red embarrassment crawls up my neck. And now's the time to prove I really do have twelve years on the sister who was too young to fight back when I left home.

"I'm sorry, Geena," I say to her. "It's been a bad day. Not that a bad day is a good excuse, but . . ." I trail off.

"*Your* day was bad," Geena says, then Dylan grabs her hand and squeezes it.

"Gee?" he asks, a pleading note in his voice.

She bites her lip. "I'm sorry, too," she says, practically under her breath.

Dylan turns to me. "Wichita? Would you mind driving us home? Please? Your mom was right. I don't have a license."

I'm too surprised by the polite request to ask why he drove to Chicago in the first place and—if he can't legally drive—whose car is sitting in front of my building. "Okay," I say instead. "I'll do it."

But I know I'm going to be sorry I did.

"I don't want to get pulled over," I said.

"You won't. Not out here."

We were on a gravel road about three miles outside Hove. Jonah—newly licensed and full of himself—was teaching me how to drive. Since I was the only sixteen-year-old in the school who hadn't been allowed to get a learner's permit, sitting behind the wheel of the ancient LiaKos Oldsmobile tasted like freedom turned into a chocolate milkshake. It tasted good.

Until I nearly wrecked the car by stepping on the gas rather than the brake.

Sitting across the road and staring at the fence posts, I felt frustration boil up inside of my chest. "I'm never getting out of this town," I said.

Jonah didn't laugh. "I did that the first time," he said. "You'll get used to it."

"I almost wrecked the car."

"You spun out on gravel," he said. "That's not even close to wrecking it. Just back up and try again."

I backed up and got the car's nose headed in the right direction—down the road rather than across it.

When I said I wasn't "allowed" to get a learner's permit, I wasn't being strictly honest. Dad said I could, but he never seemed to get around to doing more than talking about how he'd have to teach me "which side of the road was which." Mom said I had two legs and I knew how to use them. Which wasn't exactly a prohibition on learning. So I wasn't really breaking any rules by letting Jonz teach me how to drive, but if I wrecked the car and we got caught . . . well, that would be a different story.

A tractor attached to what looked like a mile-wide row of discs appeared over the top of the hill in front of us. The gravel road couldn't be more than a few feet wide. I panicked.

"Just pull over to the edge of the road and stop," Jonah said in response to my incoherent noises.

I stepped on the gas.

"The brake," Jonz moaned as we careened up the hill toward the shining row of discs.

I braked. Sliding—just a little—into the grassy ditch.

The tractor sidled by, the farmer shaking his head in disgust.

Jonah looked just the tiniest bit pale, but he started laughing after the tractor disappeared over the next low hill.

I gripped the wheel hard. Squishing the raised bumps on its back between my fingers. "When I can drive out of this place," I said, "I'm never coming back."

"Never" doesn't take into account those vague feelings of familial responsibility that can drag a person back to a birthplace once every few years. A funeral. Christmas (on those rare occasions when you can't think up a decent excuse to avoid it). I've been back to Hove exactly twice. Never—there's that word again—for more than forty-eight hours.

Now I'm driving a car—a stranger's car, since I still haven't figured out just whose car it is—past the crumpled ruins of a broken-down windmill and the all-too-correctly-modified sign.

WELCOME TO SHIT HOLE.

I'm driving back to a place I don't call home.

And I know I'm going to be sorry I did.

Chapter 15

Once upon a time, I was getting coffee in the museum break room and I overheard Kenny and Dorothy talking about Thanksgiving plans. Apparently, from what I could overhear—not that I was trying to overhear or anything—neither of them had family within easy visiting distance.

"It makes me lonely," Dorothy said, "even though I've got Joey and the twins. When I see cars of people on the freeway and I know they're driving somewhere to spend the holidays with their family, it makes me lonely."

Kenny grunted.

"They look so happy, and I just envy them getting the chance to sit down with everyone and eat turkey and stuffing."

"Mom makes the best pumpkin pie," Kenny said.

Pulling up to the white house of my childhood—complete with peeling picket fence—I wish I could do one of those *Freaky Friday* things with Dorothy. I could walk around the museum and puke in the bathroom, and she could listen to Mom.

"How could you *do* this to me?" Mom says. Screeches.

Home sweet home.

Nothing has changed. Well, that's not exactly the case. Mom's hair is a little whiter, and she's traded in the pink housedresses for pink sweats. The sweatshirt has little red hearts running in a Charlie Brown band around the middle. The bottoms are too tight for the bottom they contain. Small-town style at its best.

When we pulled up, Mom descended. A pink locust swarm. So far, she hasn't noticed me, but I've been hiding behind the trunk lid, pretending to dig bags out of the back of the car.

Geena picks up her backpack from the sidewalk where I've—graciously—tossed it.

I'm still bitter about being here.

"I didn't do anything to you," she says to Mom.

"This is all your fault," Mom says.

I automatically think she's talking to me, and I'm getting ready to defend myself when I realize she's in Dylan's face.

"This is all your fault."

I sat on a chair in the kitchen and tried to stop the blood from running down my leg and onto the floor. "Leave him alone, Mom," I said.

A hot summer's night and a conversation about stars, God, and horoscopes had given me the urge to run up and down the bleachers at the football field. Things had been going great until my toe just missed one of the wooden slats and I'd gone sliding, sliding, smashing down in between the seats. A splintered edge had connected nicely with my calf, driving a sliver—sliver is a euphemism for the log it felt like—deep into flesh.

"You'd better hope there's a God," Jonah had said as he helped me stumble off the bleachers and limp home. "Somebody has to take care of you."

"That's what you're for."

He didn't smile.

It wasn't much of a joke.

I'd been hoping Mom would already be in bed. No such luck. She was eating Pecan Sandies—Baby Geena beside her, rocking back and forth, fast asleep in her baby swing—and watching TV.

"Oh, God," Mom said when she saw my leg. Then she turned on Jonz. "This is all your fault."

"Leave him alone, Mom," I said. But it came out funny because I'd just used the junk-drawer pliers to yank the log out of my leg. Blood got on the floor.

"This is what happens when you run around all over town," Mom said as she handed me a towel. "People get hurt."

"*I* got hurt," I said. "Just me."

Somehow that wasn't the right thing to say. It wasn't a defense, but a cue for Mom to get in Jonz' face. Screaming something about . . . dirt and corruption. I don't know. I don't remember *what* she said, exactly, but the tone made me angry and I got between them and I *shoved* . . .

Not exactly. Not exactly shoved her. I hadn't intended to push her, but my leg was all Jell-O and the floor was slippery with blood and I sort of ran into her trying to get between her and Jonz.

She staggered back, falling into the table. We stared at each other, and we probably looked pretty funny because her mouth was open and I think mine was, too.

"*What* did you just do?" she asked, but it wasn't the kind of question that needed an answer.

I cringed, waiting for the slap that never came.

It wasn't restraint. The slap didn't come because Mom was restraining herself. No. She *couldn't* slap me. Because Jonz stopped her by getting in the way. He was already taller than she was, but he didn't do anything to her or threaten her. Just stepped in front of me and said, "Mrs. Gray . . . please. She's hurt."

And Mom stared up at him and her face went all pale and tight and . . . frightened.

"This is all your fault," she whispered, but it didn't sound like she was talking to Jonah at all.

"This is all your fault," Mom says to Dylan.

"Leave him alone," Geena yells, doing a pretty good imitation of Mom's screeching. "Just leave him alone."

"Geena," Dylan says, touching her shoulder. "It's all right."

"Go," Mom says to him. "Go home. You've already caused enough trouble around here."

He leaves, but not before Geena grabs his face and kisses him. Mom turns as red as the hearts on her sweatshirt. It's Geena's teenage equivalent of sticking out a defiant tongue at parental authority. Then the sidewalk is empty of teen bodies, and it's open season on Wichita.

Only nothing happens.

Mom is looking at the car. "Isn't that the Olsons' Chevy?" she asks.

I slam the trunk lid. "I don't know. It's the car they drove to Chicago in."

Mom turns her attention to me. "You've grown," she says.

"No. Same as I was five years ago."

"You're taller."

I shake my head. "Could be the shoes."

She looks down at my platform boots. "You shouldn't drive in those," she says. "They aren't safe."

I shrug. "We got here okay."

"And now I suppose you're going to turn around and leave," she says. "Leave me with this mess your sister made."

That's the plan.

The words form in my head, in my mouth, but I don't let them out.

Mom has lines around her eyes and the skin under her chin is sagging with exhaustion. "Where's Dad?" I ask instead.

"At work. Someone has to pay the bills around here." Only that last part comes out with the tiniest bit of . . . something. It's what Dad always says when he uses the good hands of Allstate as an excuse to get out of the house. Or out of something uncomfortable. *"Someone has to pay the bills around here."* Mom never says it.

I nod. "Oh."

"It's cold," she says. "I'm going inside."

I pick up my bag and follow her.

No matter how long I stay away, the house in Hove never seems to get any smaller. India always tells me how everything at her grandparents' home seems smaller now than when she was a kid. The kitchen sink used to be over her head, and now it's down around her knees. She practically falls *into* the toilet because it's so low. When I left this house, the kitchen sink came to my hip bones. It still does. The table looks just as empty, the living room just as crowded, each step on the stairs is the same distance apart from the step above and below. . . . It doesn't seem to matter how long I stay away or what height my apartment sinks have, the house on Maple Street never changes.

The curtains are even the same.

I set my bag on the floor by the kitchen door—maybe I'm hoping for a quick retreat, I couldn't say—and go to the never changing sink and pour myself a glassful of water in one of the green, plastic glasses I liked at age five. Sipping water, I stare out the window at the backyard. It's a gray day in the gray state of Illinois. Dead gray grass along a gray privacy fence mirrored in gray puddles of ice reflecting a gray sky.

Chicago . . . back in Chicago, Jonz is setting up the weaving exhibit. Gray wasn't a favorite color among the sons and daughters of infant

Chicago. Threads of red, blue, yellow, green . . . Jonah's hands buried in woven color.

The heater roars to life, and the overhead draft flutters the faded pink curtains around the window. I blink and reappear in the gray Hoveian world floored in speckled linoleum, with Mom on the phone talking to someone named Genevieve Olson. She hangs up.

"They say it's theirs. Dylan borrowed it. He cuts their grass, you know."

I didn't, but I nod and take another sip of water to cover my disorientation. "Should I take it back?"

"They'll send Todd over for it."

I nod again, even though I have no idea who the mysterious Todd is. Or how I'm going to get out of Hove. I imagine I'll have to rent a car, and that's going to hurt the credit card if it doesn't simply push it over the limit.

Which doesn't bode well for the future if I'm going to be another face in the unemployment line.

"Do you want something to eat?" Mom asks.

I feel nauseated, picturing myself trying to pay next month's bills if—

"Sure," I say out loud. Because cooking will give us something to do.

"Well, move over," she says, gently pushing at my arm so she can get to the sink.

It's the first time we've touched each other.

I left Hove at seventeen and didn't get within a hundred miles of the place until I was twenty-three. Even then, I only came back because Jonah asked me to go with him. His mother had died, and he didn't want to go to the funeral alone. I made the mistake of staying with my parents for the forty-eight hours we were in town. I should have stayed at a motel. A room with a smoke-scented bedspread and a toilet with a tissue band proclaiming SANITIZED FOR YOUR PROTECTION would have been more welcoming.

"You can use your old room," Mom said, "but you'll have to make up the sofa bed downstairs to sleep on."

"Okay," I said.

"I use your room as a sewing room now."

"Oh. That's nice."

I didn't bother to ask why. Mom doesn't sew. Never has, never will. She barely knows how to put a button back on when it falls off. But the point of turning my bedroom into a sewing room wasn't lost on me.

Upstairs, everything was different. The walls of my room had been painted powder pink. All my books were gone. The bed was gone. The closet had floor-to-ceiling stacks of boxes and all the furniture except the vanity—where the new sewing machine sat, gathering dust—had disappeared.

The window I'd crawled through to meet Jonz more times than I could count had been nailed shut.

"I gave it all to Goodwill," Mom said from behind me.

I shrugged and ignored the pepper juice stinging in my eyes. "I'm sure they were glad to have it."

"*You* certainly weren't using it."

"No." I couldn't stop staring at the window. Somehow, I didn't mind all the stuffed animals—except for Pooky-Bear, who was sitting on my bed in Chicago—I didn't mind all the stuffed animals being given away. I didn't mind having all my books given to the Goodwill where at least some other kid would get to read them. I didn't even mind having all the secret code messages I'd scribbled on the inside of my closet door painted over.

But I minded the window.

"I guess you'll have to hang up any clothes you want hung up down in the laundry room," Mom said. "There's no room in the closet."

"Okay," I said.

"It's nice having an extra room. For company."

"And for sewing."

Silence. "That, too," she said, after a bit.

And after convincing each other that we couldn't care less about the empty room, she left me to "settle in." There wasn't much settling in to do with nowhere to sleep and nowhere to hang the navy dress I'd brought for the funeral. So I went over to the vanity and took out the center drawer. I didn't open it, I took it *out*. Then, kneeling down, I looked up through the support slats to the underside of the vanity's top.

And there it was.

A pack of cigarettes, neatly taped where it wouldn't be noticed and wouldn't bump into anything inside the drawer.

I smiled for the first time since passing Hove's city limits.

"What on earth are you doing?" Mom asked from the door of the room.

I reached up between the slats and pulled the yellowed tape free of the wood. Standing up, I walked across the room, reached down for Mom's hand, and laid the pack on her palm. "You missed this," I said.

It was the first time we'd touched each other in six years.

"Well, move over," Mom says, gently pushing at my arm so she can get to the sink.

It's the first time we've touched each other.

"Why don't you take your bag up to your room?" she says as she washes her hands.

I hesitate. "Maybe I'll just stay downstairs. Since that's where I'll be sleeping."

I haven't seen the interior of my old bedroom since I placed the pack in Mom's hand. Four or five years ago, I—sort of—came back to Hove for Christmas. A big mistake, but it had been a cold, dry winter in Chicago, and day after day of below-zero temps with no snow had turned me all maudlin. After checking out a *So You Feel Maudlin Lately?* self-help book from the library, I'd decided to see if I could embark on some self-discovery by "immersing" myself in the "vibes of my childhood." I gave in to Mom's tears about familial holiday responsibility. I arrived in Hove on Christmas Eve.

I left before the ham had time to get cold.

Back in Chicago, I "immersed" the self-help book in the "vibes" of some poor schmuck's barrel fire. The library charged me sixty dollars for the privilege of losing the useless piece of trash.

I signed that sixty-dollar check with a little smiley face on the memo line.

I don't intend to try immersion again.

"It'll be easier to sleep downstairs," I say.

"If that's what you want," Mom says, pink-covered bottom sticking out of the fridge as she roots around down in the vegetable crisper. "You won't get much privacy in there, what with the play-offs."

That would be the countdown to the Final Four. Basketball, in other words. "I didn't know there was a game tonight," I say.

"Tonight and tomorrow."

I don't intend to be here tomorrow.

"No problem," I say.

"After you get settled in," Mom says, ignoring me, "come back and cut up this celery, would you?"

I'm taking my frustrations out on the innocent celery stalks, thunking the knife down onto the cutting board that fits over the kitchen sink and imagining green vegetable screams. Outside the window, starlings have turned the yard black as they fight over a puddle of ice the late afternoon sun has turned to water. Lucy, the immortal cat from next door, skulks under the barberry hedge. Belly low, she scuttles toward a clump of tall grass, which provides the next best cover. A starling sitting on a low branch catches sight of the cat and squawks. The other starlings leave the ground in a cresting wave, and Lucy pounces on a nervous cardinal that was too stupid to take the hint.

Behind me, I hear Geena come into the kitchen.

"Have you ever noticed that Lucy never catches starlings?" I ask her.

"No. Should I care?"

"Guess not." I chop off some more celery heads. Just call me the Queen of Hearts. Or was that Spades? Anyway, the one who played croquet with a bird for a mallet.

"Where's Mom?" Geena asks, popping the top on a can of Coke. Automatically, I glance at the clock. Old habits die hard. It's five oh one, but it's not my business.

"I know what time it is," Geena says, correctly reading my glance.

"How special." I scrape the chopped celery into the onions and butter in the skillet. Olive oil is an alien concept in Hove. In this house, anyway.

"I asked you where Mom is," she says.

Outside, a car door slams.

"Oh, good," Geena says, "Dad's home."

I put the cutting board into the sink and turn on the tap to wash off any stray celery remains.

Dad shuts the kitchen door behind him and returns Geena's hug. Then he wags a finger in her face and says, "You scared your mother half to death."

A direct contradiction to the sound of his voice on the phone yesterday. But that's Dad. Always cool. Always unconcerned. Always ready to sell somebody security.

He looks exactly the same. Same brown pants, same brown tie, same brown hair. Only now his hair has that Just For Men flat look to it. I wonder if Dolores does the dye job or if he brushes it into his hair while standing in front of the silvered bathroom mirror upstairs.

Dad squeezes my shoulders and gives me a kiss on the cheek. All very tidy and neat and proper. "How are you, Wichita?" he asks, as if we'd eaten pancakes together just this morning.

"Hi, Dad."

Then he surprises me. "It's nice to have you back," he says. Before the surprise can even register, he turns to Geena. "Who wants to watch the pregame show?"

"Me!" she says. And she smiles the biggest smile I've seen all week.

Later, eating spaghetti in front of the TV and grabbing my glass of decaf iced tea every time the favored team makes a basket and Dad and Geena rock the card table with their cheers, I feel like I'm looking at my childhood on some horrid reality TV show. Not that I liked basketball or even watched sports with my dad. But every time the glasses wobble, my mom flinches and looks down at the rug. Geena pretends not to notice. Dad manages to look like he's not bumping the card table on purpose.

Nothing changes in this house.

Except for my window.

Chapter 16

After the game is over and everyone's gone to bed, I sneak a peek at the telephone directory and find the closest car rental. The only car rental. It has a rather ominous name. No, not the franchise. The rental is one of the usual national franchises. But this particular franchise is owned by someone named Scaletti. It looks like Filthy Jeff or one of his relatives decided to support the local economy. The place opens at eight tomorrow morning, so I can get out of this house—this town—before anyone is awake enough to stop me.

The sofa bed is practically rusted shut, so after tugging and jerking and pinching my fingers a few times, I collapse, wheezing, onto the unopened couch. I really have to give up smoking. No twenty-eight-year-old should wheeze after a short battle with a stubborn piece of furniture. I lie on my back and stare at the ceiling, picturing various versions of black lung or whatever it is that smokers get. Positive reinforcement never worked for me. All those self-building affirmations. "I am a wonderful person." "I am cigarette-free." "I have nice breath and my teeth are white." Never worked. Not even a little bit.

Negative reinforcement is a waste, too, since the black-lung images aren't doing the trick. My fingers are twitching, and I know exactly what the nicotine hit will feel like. Maybe, instead of positive or negative affirmations (can you *have* negative affirmations?), they should teach you how to have a mentally induced nicotine rush. "Okay, people," a perky man in exercise tights will say, "picture that nicotine entering your bloodstream. C'mon, now. In-*hale! Feel* the burn." Yeah. Works for me.

Not really.

I'll quit tomorrow.

I don't want to turn on any lights, so I blindly fumble for the dead bolt on the kitchen door. Once located, the rest is easy. My fingers recognize the shape and feel of the lock. Sitting on the butt-freezing cement steps, I try to enjoy the stabilizing nicotine hit. It's hard, because from where I sit I can see the tree I used for an elevator back when my window wasn't nailed shut. If I squint through the smoke, I can even see Jonz and I sharing that first cigarette. Well, maybe not his first, but my first. The one and only bad habit Jonz ever taught me, since standing in front of freight trains never caught on.

Thinking about Jonz makes my chest hurt. It might just be the smoke and the cold, dry air, but it feels more like a heart amputation. All I wanted was to be free. To not repeat the mistakes of my parents. To exist as an individual. I *guess* that's what I'm doing. Existing.

"Have you ever wondered why we're here?" Jonz asked the day I painted my name on the windmill and declared myself immortal. We were sitting on his bed, listening to the rain rattle the roof over our heads. On the way home from the windmill, dark clouds and lightning had taken over the blue sky. We'd gotten soaked after stopping to buy two cans of Coke from the vending machines lining the outside wall of the grocery store.

I scrubbed a borrowed towel over my head and thought about his question.

"You mean like whether or not God planned it or if it was evolution?" I asked, wrapping my hair in the towel and leaning back against the faded striped wallpaper. Outside the windows, lightning snapped from the black clouds and rain ran down the glass in rivers. I closed my eyes and breathed in Jonah's room. So different from mine. Windows from floor to ceiling, peeling wallpaper, a squeaky brass bed, wood floors, and a white dresser. Nothing more. It seemed so clean compared to my room. Mom was always buying me pink sheets or some piece of delicate girly furniture. Almost as if she thought she could make me into the girl she wanted by surrounding me with all the proper embellishments.

"No, not that complicated," Jonah said. "More like, do we have a purpose or is everything just up to us?"

I took a sip of Coke. "Sounds like the same question to me. God directs us or we live to exist."

He stretched his arms over his head, then linked his hands behind his neck. "It isn't. The same question, I mean. If it were, the only way your existence could have purpose would be if you believed in some sort of divine intervention."

I thought it over. "So you want to know if our lives could have meaning without some kind of master plan?"

"Yeah. Something like that."

"Do you think Hans needs a master plan?" I asked. Hans was the German shepherd mix who had replaced the shaggy, happy-to-barf Shep from our grade school days. Hans had a nasty habit of biting anyone but me or a LiaKos, so he wasn't the constant, about-town companion old Shep had been, but he was lying between us on the bed and he looked up when I said his name.

Jonz didn't say, *"Hans is just a dog"* or any of the stupid things Mom's pastor always said whenever a kid asked if dogs went to heaven. The pastor always sent the kid home crying after saying something about dogs not having a soul so when they died, they just ceased to exist. Not like people, who had souls and went to live with Jesus. Unless they were bad.

Then they went to the devil. Whatever. Jonz didn't say any of those things. He just looked at Hans.

"I don't know if he *needs* a plan or if he's just got one. I mean, why did he end up here?" he asked.

"I think he jumped up," I said.

Jonz glared at me.

"I'm not joking," I said. "I think he made the decision to jump up, so here he is."

Hans looked from me to Jonah and back again. He wagged his tail.

"See? He agrees with me," I said, gesturing toward the tail with my Coke can.

"So you don't think it matters *why* we exist. We still make all our own decisions."

"Yeah," I said. "For good *or* evil."

I didn't amputate Jonah from my life in order to hurt him. It wasn't that I wanted to cut out my own heart. I just wanted to see if I could exist without him.

It was my own decision. For good or evil. In a perfect world, I think I'd be happier about being able to make my own decisions.

I grind the cigarette out beneath my heel, then—out of habit—bury the dead butt in the mulch around Mom's roses. If I could dig down through eleven years of archaeological layers, I would find several hundred butts from stolen summer evenings sitting on these very steps. Standing up, I slip back through the door and wrap myself up tight in the blanket I dug out of the hall closet before my attempt to open the sofa bed. I don't even bother to take off my clothes before collapsing onto the unopened couch. Morning will be here soon. And by morning, I'll be gone.

• • •

It's still dark when my internal clock wakes me from a restless, nightmare kind of sleep. If smoking dogs trying to sell me used rental cars can be called a nightmare. More like a jumble of idiot images.

I packed my bag last night, right after supper, although "packed" is a loose term since I never really took anything out but my toothbrush and a pair of socks. I fold the blanket, pull on my shoes, then slip through the winter's dawn dimness into the kitchen.

And stop.

Have you ever had the feeling that you aren't alone? Walking home late at night, heels clicking on the sidewalk, and suddenly you get the creeping sensation up the back of your neck that makes you turn around to see if there's someone behind you? Well, there's someone in the kitchen. Sitting in the dark at the little table by the window. My not-so-amputated heart begins to bang around in my ribs as I try to see who or what is in the room. *"Always look to the side of what you want to see,"* Jonah used to tell me. There. A darker darkness just moved.

"Mom?" says a small voice I only recognize because I heard it back when it came from the mouth of a baby girl.

"Geena?" I ask, turning on the light and blinking in the glare. "It's Wichita."

"I don't feel good," Geena says, still sounding about three years old.

I look at the back door. It smiles at me and beckons me outside and down freedom road. Okay, so Geena's got the flu. *"Is that really your problem?"* the smiling door asks.

I look back at Geena. She's got her head cradled on her arms and she's white. Really white.

Then I see the blood.

"Ah, Jesus," I say, because I can't think of anything else to say.

• • •

"I think I'd like that," Jonz said. "Knowing that my decisions were my own even if they turned out all wrong."

I shrugged and the borrowed towel slipped off my head and landed in a wet heap on Hans' tail. Hans gave me an unhappy look.

"I thought you didn't believe in gods or horoscopes," I said to Jonah while giving Hans a pat of apology.

"I don't."

"Then why wouldn't your decisions be your own?"

He looked at me for one moment. Two. I would have known what he was thinking if his thoughts weren't so tangled up in his eyes.

"Because I'm worried," he said finally. "Worried that I have to repeat all the mistakes of my parents."

I scowled. "That's dumb."

"Geena!" I shake my sister's shoulder. She feels cold under my hand.

Jesus. God. What's going on?

"Mom!" I scream, hoping my voice will carry up the stairs and through the little sound machine Mom uses to drown out Dad's snores and the squeaks and moans the house makes at night. Something thumps on the floor overhead. As if a body fell out of bed. "Mom," I call again. "I need your help, Mom."

I'm looking for injuries. Suicide? Geena's wrists are smooth and white. So the blood is coming . . .

Ah, hell.

"Wichita?" Mom yells down the stairs. "Is that you?"

"In the kitchen." I reach for the phone.

Mom comes in just as the 911 operator answers the phone.

"Oh, sweet Jesus," Mom says, falling onto her knees beside Geena.

"A medical emergency," I say in response to the operator's query.

Address? I start to give my address in Chicago. No, wait. Maple Street. Will I be here when the ambulance arrives? Yes, dammit, I'm her sister. Someone will be there right away.

People I know who've been in emergencies always tell me that time expands. Things move more slowly. A lifetime occurs in a single minute. I must be an odd duck. Because the morning's events flip by like a fast-forwarded VHS tape. People talk, but their heads bounce from side to side and their mouths move at an accelerated rate. Everyone has to say sentences to me twice. Repeat the play in slow motion so I can understand what's going on.

"It's a miscarriage. She's in shock," Mom says to me for the second time as we sit in the emergency waiting area of Hove General. I asked her to repeat the sentence even though I'd already guessed what was going on this morning before I called 911.

"How do you know?" I ask.

Mom looks down at the linoleum floor. It's white with blue flecks. "Isn't it obvious?"

Isn't *what* obvious? I look at the floor, too. Across from us, Dad shifts in his chair. The chairs are deliberately uncomfortable. That way, only people who are bleeding to death or who have dropped into a coma will stay put. Everyone else will get up and leave, deciding that pneumonia or a broken arm is less painful than sitting on these chairs, waiting to see the doctors.

I glance up at the security camera focused on me. Somewhere, upstairs, there's a doctors' lounge with a video feed so the doctors can watch people shift and squirm. I'm willing to put money on it. *"I'll bet that bum is numb,"* is probably the running joke. Either that or they're busy posting bets with the lounge bookie. *"The broad in chair number three. She won't hold out more than ninety minutes."*

Dad shifts again. Crosses his legs. Uncrosses them. I look up from his shoes to his face. He's looking at Mom. And the corner of his mouth bounces around from a smile to a smirk to a frown. He catches me looking at him and he stands up. The movement is too fast, and I end up staring at his belt buckle so I don't see what the corner of his mouth is doing when he says, "Well, I'd better get to work. Someone has to pay the bills around here."

"It's Saturday, Brad," Mom says. Very quiet.

A nurse on her way through to the station pauses to look at Dad's face. She's standing in between Mom and Dad, or I think Mom might have pounced on him. Like Lucy the immortal cat pounced on the unsuspecting cardinal.

"Lots of work to do," Dad says. "Even on Saturday. Give me a call when you have news." Then he's gone. But not before I see genuine fear and a banked-campfire kind of anger in the twitching corner of his mouth. Not fear of Mom pouncing on him. Fear of something else. Hospitals, maybe. I've only seen him in a hospital twice. When Geena was born and when Grandma died. I really have no way of knowing if he's scared of hospitals or not. Maybe he's just missing a backbone.

"Next time," Grandma said to me, "pick a man with a little backbone. Grow one yourself!"

I stared at her.

Grandma—my mom's mother—had Alzheimer's. We didn't know she had Alzheimer's until I was ten or so. Up to that point, Mom thought she deliberately forgot things just to ruin Mom's life. Everyone wanted to ruin Mom's life in those days. From the grocery store when it ran out of Sandies to the post office when it delivered mail for a house on Maplewood Drive rather than Maple Street . . . to Dad.

It always came back to Dad.

Ten was somewhere between the time Mom lectured me about sex and the time I went on my first date with Filthy Jeff. I was a nonentity in those few short years. Too young to get into any *real* trouble. Too old to require constant supervision. But every Saturday afternoon, Mom and I went to Grandma's house.

Grandma's house was actually an apartment in the assisted-living facility on the south edge of town. The facility had all the homey character of a prison camp. Grandma hadn't always lived there. I have vague memories of a small house surrounded by trees and smelling of old linens and Pledge. Less vague memories of a window ledge lined with bottles made of blue, green, yellow, and red glass. I liked playing in the colors when the sun shown through that window. I think these vague memories are Grandma's house, but I've never had the courage to ask Mom if they are real memories or memories of a dream.

I never saw brightly colored bottles in Grandma's apartment. And it smelled like bleach and bathroom air freshener. The kind of air freshener you find in truck stop restrooms. Industrial strength.

"Hi, Mama," Mom always said as she gave Grandma a kiss on the cheek.

Grandma stared at the TV.

I tugged on Mom's hand. "Can I go play in the rec room?" The rec room had a pool table. I liked rolling the balls back and forth and making baskets. I had tried a pool cue once, but it had dug up a little divot of green cloth. Frightened of being punished—or worse, banished from the rec room—I'd left the pool cue on the table and run back to Grandma's apartment. But no one ever found the divot. So I felt safe as long as I didn't use a cue.

"Say hello to your grandma," Mom said instead of answering.

"Hi, Grandma."

Grandma looked at me and said, "Your mother is weak and your father is a coward. Too bad for you, little girl!" Then she smiled. "How are you, dear?"

It was a little like having a spirit medium for a relative. Just enough truth to be believable. Just enough weirdness to make it dismissible.

"Fine," I said.

"Next time," Grandma said to me, "pick a man with a little backbone. Grow one yourself!"

I stared at her.

"No, not you," she said, craning her neck to look at me. Then she looked up at Mom. "Did you bring me anything?"

In the car, on the way home, I asked Mom what Grandma had meant by "a little backbone."

She didn't answer.

Staring at the chair Dad just vacated, I remember what Grandma said and I wonder if she was talking about Dad.

"Is Dad scared of hospitals?" I ask Mom.

She acts as if she hasn't heard me. Acts as if the floor is the most interesting linoleum she's seen all year. I'm just about to repeat the question when the nurse who saved Dad's bacon by getting in the middle of things sits down beside us.

"Maggie," the nurse says, "I haven't seen you in ages. How is everything?"

"*Gee, I dunno. We're just sitting here in the emergency room for laughs so the doctors can bet on our bum numbness.*" I can hear my teeth click as I bite down on the words that almost make it out of my fast-forward mouth.

But the nurse isn't really asking.

Mom adjusts her attention from the floor to the nurse. She goes very still, almost as if she recognizes the perky face under the white cap.

"Just like old times, huh?" the nurse says, patting Mom's knee. "She'll be all right. No harm done."

And despite the accelerated time warp I'm in, I still catch the malicious glitter in the nurse's pretty blue eyes.

Just like old times, huh?

"Wichita," Mom says to me, even though she's still looking into the nurse's glittering eyes. "Wichita, go call Dylan."

Chapter 17

Dylan.

Time speeds up, then slows down, leaving me with whirligig nausea.

How could I forget Dylan?

I'm all the way to the pay phone when I realize I don't know Dylan's number or even his last name. I retrace my steps. The nurse is gone, and Mom is crying.

I've seen my mother cry for every possible reason.

Usually, I avoid being in the same room. I don't like manipulation.

"You don't love me," Mom said at the supper table.

"For God's sake, Maggie," Dad said. "I just asked for the potatoes."

Two silver tears rolled down Mom's cheeks. I stopped chewing my carrot stick and watched the tears compete with each other to reach her chin first. Two damp racehorses galloping toward the finish line.

The moment stretched. The tears met on the tip of Mom's chin, joined, hung, dripped. More took their place. Silent. Deadly.

Dad slopped potatoes onto his plate. A spoonful. Another. Another. Until his plate practically overflowed with wet chunks. "Look," he said, trying hard to make it sound like a joke, "I'm eating these potatoes. I love you, okay? Now stop crying."

The tears kept chasing each other down Mom's cheeks.

Dad threw down his spoon. "What? What did I do this time?"

"You don't love me. If you loved me, you'd be happy."

"Happy." He spit out the word.

The carrot was bitter and dry. I couldn't swallow it. I leaned over and spit it out into my napkin.

"We're having a *baby*," Mom said. "You should be happy."

"I'm happy," Dad said around a deep sigh. "Now would you stop crying?"

Mom's tears were already gone. She'd won.

Mom is crying.

But I don't know what to do with these tears.

They're for real.

Sitting down, I hesitate, then try and put my arm around her shoulders.

She shoves me. "Go away."

I pull my arm back.

"Go *away!*"

"I need Dylan's number," I say, keeping my voice soft. "I can't call him. I need a number. Or a last name."

"Thomas," she says, still not looking at me. "His father is Richard or Rick or something."

I start to walk back to the phone before I realize . . .

"Mom," I say, standing in front of her again. "Dylan Thomas? Are you sure?"

She glares at me around red eyes. "What do you mean?"

"The poet?"

Confusion. "What?"

"Never mind," I say.

It's Saturday. Dylan is doing snow removal. Somewhere. The east side, maybe? Am I a new or old customer?

"Snow?" I ask.

"Only a foot of it. Where've you been?"

"I'm Geena's—his girlfriend's—sister," I say. "Geena's had . . . in the hospital." I don't know if Dylan's parents know about Geena. About the baby. In the background I can hear the roadrunner outwit the coyote. A child screams. The woman I'm talking to—she sounds too young to be Dylan's mother—says something to the child. Then:

"Geena's sick?"

"Um . . . yeah."

"The baby? Is the baby all right?"

"You know about the baby?" I ask.

"Of course I know about the baby. It's my first grandchild. Why wouldn't I know about the baby?"

Not too young.

And nothing like my mother.

"Geena's had a miscarriage," I say, trying to make my voice sound gentle, even if the words aren't.

"Mary, Mother of God," Dylan's mother says. "We'll be right over."

"How come I don't have any aunts or uncles?" I asked Mom one afternoon when I was helping her plant nursery flats of petunias in the front window boxes. Maybe it was after one of our weekly visits to Grandma. I think it was a spring day during the time when I was somewhere between nine and twelve. (Geena wasn't born yet.) The nonentity years.

"Because Grandma didn't have any other children," Mom said as she dug into the dirt with a trowel.

"Doesn't Dad have any brothers or sisters?"

"No."

I stuck a petunia plug into the dirt.

"Not like that," Mom said. "That's crooked. Make it straight and tall so it will reach for the sun."

I replanted the petunia.

"I wish we had a big family," I said. "Like Jonah's. He's got brothers and a sister and aunts and uncles and cousins—"

Mom stabbed the trowel into the dirt. "Why don't you go find something else to do and stop bothering me."

I ran all the way to Jonah's house. The wind dried any tears I might have cried.

"Wichita?"

At first it sounds like Jonz, but when I turn around, it's Dylan. He's wearing a jacket and jeans and he's covered in snow. His chest is heaving, and I realize the hospital is on the east edge of town.

"Is she okay?" he asks. Gasps.

I nod. "She's okay now. Mom's in with her."

"The baby?"

I try to say something, but my mind is a painful blank. Didn't his mother tell him? Then I can see that she did. He just wants her to be wrong.

"Oh, God." He sits down. Drops of melting snow and tears fall onto the floor. I sit down beside him and catch his cold, bare hand . . . not sure if I should touch him or if . . .

He wraps his arms around me and sobs into my chest. "She's all right," he says. "I was scared. . . . I thought maybe . . ."

"She's okay," I say into his snow-wet hair. I can smell ice and fear and sadness.

"Dylan, honey." A small woman who doesn't look any older than me sits down on the other side. She gives me a quick smile, then returns her attention to Dylan.

Over Dylan's head and the stranger's—Dylan's mother's—shoulder, I can see a crowd of people who vaguely resemble the boy in my arms. Adults, children, even a grandma or two. One by one, they hug Dylan or—if they can't reach all of him—stretch a hand through to pat him on the shoulder or knee.

"Geena?" Dylan's mother asks me. "Can we see her?"

I know Mom is going to hate this—even more than the perky, malicious-eyed nurse who is flapping her hands uselessly at the door of Geena's room—but I take them all in at once.

They're Geena's family.

Even if she doesn't know it yet.

"I wish I had a big family," I said to Jonah, after running all the way to his house and leaving my mother to plant her petunias alone.

"No, you don't," he said. He was scraping the dirt from around the roots of an oak tree. The tree sat on a hill that had been cut away to form the LiaKoses' driveway. In the dirt of the cut, the roots formed a network of mountain roads for our Matchbox cars and plastic jeeps and trucks. We'd borrowed—okay, stolen—an old spoon from his mother's silverware drawer, and I was using it to dribble sand from the sandbox onto the roads Jonz was scraping away with his pocketknife.

"Yes, I do," I said. "I want a *big* family. Even bigger than yours. You've only got Zeke and Caro and Craig—"

"Sure," he said. "And you want hand-me-down clothes, no bicycle for your birthday, and fighting over the TV every Saturday morning."

I thought about it. "I wouldn't have to wear hand-me-downs. I'm the oldest."

"Whoop-dee-doo. Put some sand here." He pointed to a steep road.

I sprinkled the sand, then smoothed it out with a finger. "It looks like a real road. If you squint."

We stepped back and squinted.

"Okay," I said. "I don't want brothers and sisters. I still wish I had a lot of cousins, and aunts and uncles who'd give me presents at Christmas. But most of the time, it'd just be me and Mom and Dad."

Jonz dug at the dirt above the next root.

"You know?" I asked. "That way I could watch what I wanted on Saturdays. Most of the time. Except Christmas."

He kept digging.

"You know?"

He threw the knife down and ran into the house.

I picked it up and brushed it off. It was his favorite thing, and he wouldn't want it to get ruined. I followed him into the house. He was sitting in the big chair in front of the TV and watching a little-kid TV show.

"You dropped your knife," I said.

"Go away and leave me alone."

Crowded together against the wall by the hospital room's bathroom, Mom whispers to me, "Who *are* these people? Geena's still weak. The doctor said—"

"They're a family who loves each other," I say, all nasty and sarcastic, only to feel sorry the next moment because of the sad, hurt look that crosses her face. "They're Dylan's family."

She ponders the meaning for a bit, then whispers again. "Do they know? About . . ." She waves a hand in the general direction of the bed.

It takes me a second or two to understand that she means the baby. Mom still—even after the entire emergency room staff just finished pumping enough blood into her daughter to save her from going into shock—

Mom still can't say the word "baby." As if somehow even the word—unsanctified by holy matrimony—is filthy.

"They know," I say. Then, making it even more blunt, I add, "They *already* knew."

She turns as red as the cardinal Lucy caught. Puffs out her feathers. "She told *them*, but she didn't tell *me*? Her own *mother*?"

One of the grandmas hears Mom's raised voice and turns, smiles. I don't think she understood what Mom was saying, just happened to hear voices and notice we were there. She gestures to Mom. A "come be a part of this" kind of gesture.

"Maybe Geena needed love rather than a lecture," I say, smiling at Grandma.

I add the last bit just to hurt Mom. I'm tired, I'm cranky, and I want to go back to Chicago.

If Mom is a failure, what does that make me?

After Jonz told me to leave him alone, I ran to the outcrop. The outcrop was a pile of rocks pushed up out of the soil by tree roots and water. Jonah and I had found it one day while we were exploring the hill just outside town. If you had a taste for danger, you could crawl into the dark, earthy space the rocks had left behind as they thrust up into the sunshine. I usually didn't. The thought of being crushed or buried alive under several tons of limestone didn't make the hole inviting at all. I'd only gone in once before. To show Jonz that I wasn't chicken. But today, nobody wanted me. So maybe it would serve them all right if the earth swallowed me up.

Flopping down on my belly, I crawled into the hole. It had been a dry spring. A good thing, or I would have been sitting in water. There was enough room to pull my knees to my chest and, if I kept my chin on my knees, I could sit up and see out of the hole I'd just crawled through.

Beyond the frame of rock, the grass and the tops of the trees farther on down the hill waved in the spring wind.

Nobody wanted me.

I didn't have a family.

I just had people who wanted me to die and leave them alone.

Somewhere in the middle of the self-pity, I heard something scratching outside the hole. Then Jonah's face appeared in the rock frame.

We looked at each other. I couldn't see his face since his back was to the western sun. He probably couldn't see me because of the shadows in the hole. But we looked at each other. And even though I couldn't see his face, I've always remembered what he looked like. As if I *did* see him somehow.

"I'm sorry, Cheetah."

I squeezed my eyes shut. The apology didn't feel good at all. It hurt just as much as being told to leave him alone. Because Dad always said he was sorry, too, but he didn't mean it. He just wanted everybody to smile so he could watch the basketball game without feeling guilty. Maybe Jonah just wanted to watch TV without feeling guilty.

"I don't want you to go away," Jonz said.

I kept my eyes shut.

"Do you want to come out? I can go in there with you, if you want."

Maybe I didn't care if the earth fell on *me*, but there wouldn't be any moral satisfaction if we died together.

I crawled out.

We sat on one of the rocks that had toppled off the pile pushed up by the tree. It made a kind of seat just outside the hole's entrance. Jonah's arm brushed against mine. I was covered with bits of leaves, sticks, dirt, and crud. He was sweating.

He opened his fist, and I saw he was holding the pocketknife. He pulled out the spirally, pointed thing and jabbed the sharp point into his thumb. Blood globbed up. Then he reached out and took my hand.

I don't remember being afraid. I don't even remember it hurting when he stuck my thumb with the corkscrew. But his hand was warm, and the little bits of dirt and stick rubbed rough between his skin and mine.

When a drop of blood appeared, he pressed our thumbs together.

"We're family," Jonz said. "We don't need anyone else."

I'm tired, I'm cranky, and I want to go back to Chicago.

If Mom is a failure, what does that make me?

I told my family I didn't want him anymore.

I leave the hospital room and walk down the hallway and out the door. It's not snowing now. From the look of the street, it stopped snowing before I found Geena in the kitchen. I just didn't notice the foot of white stuff in the short drive to the emergency ward.

It's a long walk back to the house on Maple Street. My boots are covered with salt rime from the zealous homeowners and city utility salt and sand trucks. I read somewhere that champagne can bring the shine back to a pair of salt-ruined boots. Or was that cognac? Either way, too expensive for my discount footwear.

I pull open the gate attached to the peeling picket fence. The fence looks even dirtier against the snow that piles up behind the gate. In the yard, birds are crowded around the feeders and a small pack—flock? covey? batch?—of starlings is fighting over the last of the suet in the suet basket. From here, their squeals sound like pigs fighting over a choice bit of slop in the trough. Not that I've seen a pig since that grade school field trip to the local hog farmer's, but the sound is easy to identify and hard to forget.

I find the birdseed in the pantry, fill the feeders, replace the suet cake, and thaw the water in the birdbath. I'm watching the starlings crowd around the water when India calls.

"Good," she says when I answer. "You're not stranded on the road somewhere."

"Geena miscarried—" I say, still looking at the starlings.

"Is she all right?"

"—or I'd probably have tried to leave, snow or no snow."

India is silent.

I'm silent.

"All I do is hurt people," I say after a bit. "I can't seem to help myself. And she went into shock, but she's okay now. She has a family."

"Wichita . . ." India begins, then she trails off. "I'm glad she's okay."

I nod at my reflection in the window glass.

"Some guy named Mike called," she says. "He wanted to know where you were."

I nod again.

"Wichita?"

"Thanks," I say out loud. "I'll call him."

"Do you need some money?" India asks. "To get home, I mean. What with quitting your job—"

"How did you know about that?" I ask. "Not that I mind. Just wondering."

"Janet called. She said you'd quit. And she left a message. Hang on. . . ." She's fumbling with pins and pieces of paper. I can picture her standing next to the cork message board we hung by the phone. I hit my thumb with the hammer while pounding in the nail. Looking down, I can see a tiny scar on my thumb. Not from the hammer.

"We're family. We don't need anyone else."

"I don't want you to go away." Only it isn't Jonz' voice. It's mine.

"Here it is," India says. "'Thanks. D-Day is Monday.' Very cryptic.

Although she asked if I thought red was a good color for a first date. Do you know what it means?"

"Haven't a clue," I say.

Silence, except for the crinkling of paper as India wads up Janet's happy little entrapment message. It sounds a lot like pom-poms waved by an enthusiastic cheerleader.

"Are you sure about the money?" India asks. "I could—"

"I'll be okay," I say. I try an experimental smile at my reflection. Try to see if I can inject something pleasant into my voice by covering up all the mess in my chest with a smile. "I don't have my bowl and harmonica right now. You wouldn't want to miss out on that."

"Right," India says. "I'll keep them warm for you. Just in case you have to go begging."

Chapter 18

Hanging up the phone, I picture myself sitting on a generic sidewalk in a generic city, holding out a bowl in one hand and playing train-rolling harmonica music with the other. Harmonicas sound like freight trains if you listen just right. I lean on the sink and wonder what kind of bowl I would use. Wood? Chinese porcelain? Or would I let the music of the freight train carry me away? Just past the window, the hungry birds are cleaning up the seed I put out and tipping back beakfuls of water. Happy hour down at the Gray house. You know the place. Maple Street. The water's free and plentiful. No need to mind your p's and q's down at the Gray house.

I wonder if Mike is setting up The Club for the evening. I wonder if I should call him now or just pretend I never knew him. I remember leaning over the table—kissing him willing—and embarrassed heat warms me from sole to hair tip.

I pour myself a drink of water to cool the heat.

The birds fly off in a tipsy mob as Dad pulls into the driveway. It's harder for him to get out of the car than it used to be. He has to swing his body a little to get enough momentum going to propel himself out of the bucket seat. The swing contrasts badly with the flat brown hair.

"Wichita," he says after shutting the kitchen door. He gives my shoulders a squeeze, then takes off his coat. "Your mother called the office, and she wants some things from home."

"They're spending the night?"

He pats his chest. "The company's got a good plan. No kicking my little girl out on her ass." After digging in his shirt pocket, he hands me a slip of paper. "Here's the list."

I look down and see a scrawl of wishes. A blanket. A stuffed animal. A mug. A Bible. This isn't Geena's list.

Dad pulls a beer out of the fridge. And that's when I get it. Mom called Dad with the list, but I'm the one who's supposed to carry out the order.

"Have you been back to the hospital?" I ask, even though I know the answer.

"What?" He pops the top of the beer can. "No. I'd just be in the way." Then he sidles—there really is no other word for it—out of the kitchen. A moment later, the TV comes on and I hear the voices of the exhibitionists featured on the late-afternoon talk shows.

The sound of those voices is . . . lonely. The cries of geese flying a thousand feet above you in the dark of a winter's night. Only these TV cries don't have the romance of fall migration. They're just haunting voices of unbearable loneliness.

All day staring out the window. A car. A flight of birds. A squeeze. A pat. Three sentences. Then voices of people a thousand miles away, lost in the winter night. I stare at the coat and briefcase lying on the kitchen table.

Does Mom put that coat and briefcase away every evening before cooking supper?

I pick up the phone and call the hospital. The number is taped to the wall along with the fire department, pastor, police, and even 911. The hospital receptionist answers. I ask for Geena's room number.

The fire department, pastor, police, 911, the high school, the hair salon on Fourth Street . . .

Dad's work number isn't on the list.

"Hi, Mom," I say when Mom answers. "How's Geena?"

Silence.

"Mom?"

"Fine," she says. "Everything is fine."

"Dad just got home," I say. "He gave me a list." I read off the list. "Anything else you want me to bring?"

"Whatever you bring will be just fine." She makes it sound like she's experiencing a stoning or some other painful form of martyrdom. Arrows, maybe. Or lions. *Whatever I bring will be just fine.*

It won't be.

My new wellspring of pity just went dry.

I hunt down all the things on the list and toss them into a box along with a few oversized shirts from Geena's closet. I've never stayed in a hospital, but I've seen enough greeting cards to know that hospital gowns must be unpleasant. When I get back to the kitchen, Dad's car keys are lying on top of his briefcase. In plain view. Almost deliberate. I don't bother to ask if he wants to go with me.

The road to the hospital passes the Burger King. Someone has added landscaping. A weeping tree and lumps of dead vegetation covered in snow.

"What do you want to do with your life?" I asked Jonz as we sat down at our booth and took the burgers and fries off the tray. No one who knew anything ate off those trays. Not because of what it would look like. But because of insider knowledge. When you've seen the guy standing behind the counter stick cafeteria straws up his nose and spew milk through them two-hundred-plus days a year for the last ten years, you don't eat off the trays he's supposed to wipe down. People are supposed to outgrow the straw-milk trick. The fact that this particular specimen of humanity *didn't* is a hygienic road sign for the cautious.

"Do I have to make a decision right now?" Jonz asked, setting the trays on top of the nearest trash can.

"You're seventeen," I said.

"So?"

"Don't you pay any attention to those talks the guidance counselor gives?"

"Do you?"

Of course not. But I was working up to something. I reached into my backpack and handed Jonz the letter I'd gotten yesterday afternoon. It scared me. It excited me.

He turned it over and looked at the impressive seal. "You got in?"

I bounced a little on the molded seat, then shoved a french fry into my mouth and nodded.

"What do you know," he said. "I didn't think you could do it."

I kicked him under the table. He kicked me back. We both grinned. I wouldn't have applied to the University of Chicago at all if Jonz hadn't twisted my arm. Literally. Actually, it was more like arm wrestling. If I won, I got to apply to a junior college and feel sorry for myself. If he won, I had to apply to schools someone had actually heard of.

I may have let him win.

Jonz pulled an equally impressive envelope out of his pocket. "Dual acceptance," he said. "School of Fine Arts *and* Art History."

I grabbed at the letter. "No way!"

"Your confidence is underwhelming."

Not that he would have applied if we hadn't had another bout of arm wrestling.

That time, I won.

"What are you two squealing about?" Mr. Straws-up-His-Nose asked as he picked up the trays. "Dumb-asses."

"Hey! Dumb-ass! You parked or something?"

I blink awake and realize the left-turn arrow is green. A glance in the rearview mirror confirms that the guy behind me—the one filled with goodwill toward mankind and driving a dual-tone pickup—looks suspiciously like Mr. Straws. Does anything in this town change? Or will Mr. Straws marry and beget a bevy of little Mr. Straws who will work at Burger King and snort milk out their noses at seventeen?

I shrug off the annoyance. Somehow, being honked at, flipped off, and having your parentage questioned isn't annoying in Chicago. It's part of the game we all play with each other. In Hove, the insults feel personal.

I'd forgotten.

The hospital is a dismal affair. This morning, the emergency room had an air of deliberate disgust. A "we have to treat you, but we don't have to like you" smell. But the main wing—the visitor's entrance—is saccharine-sweet. WE'RE HERE TO SERVE YOU! the sign curving along the reception wall reads. At the visitor's entrance, everybody smiles. No shoes squeak on the carpeted floor. I could be checking in to a Holiday Inn.

All that changes when I leave the elevator on the second floor. My shoes squeak here. Nurses glare at me, and the air smells like blood and antiseptic. The box is getting heavy, and I'm glad when I set it down on the spare bed in Geena's room. Geena's back is to the door, her face to the wall. I'd think she was asleep if I thought sleepers held every muscle at alert.

Dylan and his family are nowhere in sight.

Mom sifts through the contents of the box. "Didn't you bring the magazines?" she whispers.

"What magazines?" I ask, normal voice. She hushes me with a hand. "What magazines?" I whisper. Which is kind of unnecessary since I just said it out loud, but I'm nervous.

"The ones by Geena's bed."

"They weren't on the list."

"Yes, they were."

"They weren't on the list Dad gave me."

Mom sighs. "Let me see it."

"I threw it away."

"Are you always so careless?"

"It was a list, Mom. I put everything on the list into the box, then I threw it away."

"Did you check it twice?"

Naughty or nice?

"Everything on the list is in that box," I say. "Plus some shirts."

She pulls out the shirts. "She never wears these. Why'd you bring these? They weren't on the list."

I don't stay long. I lean over Geena's stiff body and ask her how she's doing. She doesn't answer, so I say good night and I leave.

On the way home, something pulls me into the Burger King. It's not hunger. It's definitely not nostalgia for the years I spent taking orders at the drive-through. But I walk through the familiar door and I order the smallest excuse for being there I can get—fries and a drink—and I carry my tray to the booth Jonz and I always shared. Only this booth. If someone else were in it, we ate outside on the curb. The booth was tradition, custom, gospel.

I take my food off the tray and nearly drop the tray when I reach out to set it on a nonexistent trash can. The trash cans have been moved. They're by the door now. I slide my tray into the stack and smile at the guy behind the counter. He must be Mr. Straws' younger brother. Or cousin. I walk back to the booth. Look around to see if anyone is watching, then kneel down on the floor and run my fingers along the edge of the vinyl seat, just where it joins the base.

Eleven years. I'm sure things have been remodeled. Above me, flowered wallpaper has replaced paint. But maybe—

"Did you lose something?"

I jump. Hit my head on the booth table. Rubbing my dented skull, I look over at the guy who's picking up the trays. "Got it," I say, holding up a piece of convenient trash I just noticed on the floor in front of me. I stand up and throw the straw wrapper away. The guy shakes his head and hefts the trays. He might mumble "Dumb-ass" under his breath.

Sitting back down, I pretend to eat while running my fingers along the edge of the seat. My weight must have gapped the spot. I feel paper. Pull it out.

"What if . . ." I said after Mr. Straws-up-His-Nose left, "What if this is the last time we eat here?"

"It's only March."

"Yeah . . ." I trailed off.

"What are you thinking?"

I reached into my backpack and pulled out a piece of paper. "I want to leave something," I said. "Something to make a mark on the place."

Jonz set down his burger. "How?"

"There's a hole in this seat," I said. "Not a real hole. A gap."

He finished off his fries while I wrote on the paper. I handed it to him.

"'This is a paper left behind by Wichita Gray and Jonah LiaKos,'" Jonz read out loud. "Can't you change it to Jonz?" he asked.

I shook my head. "It has to be real names."

"Why?"

"Keep reading."

"'This was written on the last day we spent at Burger King our senior year.'" He snorted. "That's a lie."

"They'll never know."

"'If you find it, sign your name and put it back for the next person to find.'"

"Ta-da," I said. "Immortality."

"You're obsessed. Write a book or something."

"But this is more fun," I said. "Sort of like secret code passed down through the ages."

"Okay, I get it."

"Sign your name."

"Why? So future generations can forge my signature and get a bunch of credit cards in my name?" he teased.

I kicked him under the table. He moaned in mock agony. We were too happy, too soon-to-be free to take anything seriously. He signed his name. I signed mine. Then I folded it and put it into the crack.

By chance, that day turned out to be the last time we ate at Burger King. I worked there for three more months. But I never sat down at the booth again.

I feel paper. Pull it out.

The paper has turned yellow and soft. It unfolds more like cloth than the crisp, collegiate-lined sheet I folded up eleven years ago.

The signatures stretch from my name to the bottom of the sheet, then back up and down the other side. Name after name after name. I don't recognize any from the bottom of the sheet on until I find two near the end of the fourth column.

Geena Gray. Dylan Thomas.

I fumble in my bag for a pen. The pen hovers over the paper. Emotion flows like blood and ink, and I don't know what to say. I almost write, "Thank you," but I click the pen closed, fold up the paper, and put it back where I hid it years ago.

Outside, the melting snow falls in wet clumps from the newly planted trees.

Inside, I make water circles on the table with a melting piece of ice.

I sit in the Burger King booth until someone swipes a damp mop over my feet. The house on Maple Street is dark when I pull into the driveway. Tucking my coat around me, I sit on the porch steps—where the snow couldn't reach—and smoke an entire pack of cheap, convenience-store cigarettes. One right after the other. Until the cold and smoke and memories start to choke me.

Upstairs, I can hear my father roll over and start to snore.

Chapter 19

Dad squeezes my shoulder. I roll over and nearly roll off the couch. Blinking in the sunlight poking its head through a crack in the curtains, I can see Dad has shaved.

"Think I'll go to church," he says.

I look at the post office T-shirt (long-sleeved for winter) and the hybrid golf/wingtip shoes. "I had no idea she was ordained," I say.

Dad frowns. A moment later I hear the kitchen door slam. The car stays silent, so he must be walking. I picture him walking down the sidewalk he knows so well, walking past the winter-dead curbside gardens, walking past the yipping poodle on the corner. Walking along, rubber overshoes flapping in the snow. Walking to see Dolores like he's done a thousand times before.

I roll over and bury my face in the crack between the back and the seat of the couch and ignore the smiling sunshine poking me in the eye.

And I dream someone has installed a light over my head. Now I can have a lightbulb moment.

A lightbulb moment.

That moment when—cartoonlike—you put two and two together and come up with four instead of three.

• • •

For two weeks one summer—one of those nonentity summers that all seem to fade into one—Mom decided I needed to make cute, Barbie-loving friends rather than running around town with "that boy." And what better way to find girlfriends than to send me off to an all-girl summer camp? I think she had images of pretty, well-behaved, well-scrubbed little girls stringing beads or pouring different colors of sand into bottles. Maybe doing something as physically active as taking a hike or learning how to paddle a canoe—all belted up safely into a life jacket, of course.

The possibility of late-night, all-cabin farting contests probably didn't even cross her mind.

The flour war caused the first recognizable lightbulb moment of my cigar box life. Flour wars are standard camp fare. Happy little campers—each handed tissue packets of flour—are divided into two teams and told to run through the woods playing an only slightly less violent version of dodge ball. The team with the fewest flour spatters wins.

We pushed and shoved each other as we stood in line waiting for our flour packets. The counselor who gave me three small bundles leaned over and said, "Don't let it get into your eyes or it will blind you."

I looked down at the flour packets in my hand. No one could possibly be more cruel and sadistic than the adult who had thought up this game. Not only did it pit the athletic against the less fortunate, it obviously had permanent and horrible results if you should get flour into your eyes. I didn't want to be blind. I liked being able to see.

After throwing my packets into a bush, I spent the majority of the war cowering behind a tree. When Annie—or Muscles, as she was known to those of us who were less fortunate—found me, I covered my eyes with my hands and screamed, "Not in the face, not in the face." Annie was so surprised, her aim went wild and she hit the tree trunk. Flour sifted down over my head, but my eyes were safe.

Since I never went back to the camp—I farted at the supper table one night, demonstrating how I'd won the contest after chili night—the flour issue didn't come up again. One day, about a month or two ago—no kidding!—I was making cookies to take to work for Kenny's birthday party. A strand of hair fell into my eye and I reached up a flour-covered hand to rub it and replaced the hair with a fingerful of flour. Dry, itchy, nasty stuff that forces you to shut your eyes until the sting goes away. I was washing my face in the sink when I realized what the camp counselor had meant.

A lightbulb moment.

That moment when—cartoonlike—you put two and two together and come up with four instead of three.

Dad's insurance policy is only good for one night. The hospital bumps Geena out of her room by midafternoon. On a Sunday, no less. After five nights in a fetal position, I've gotten to like the feeling, and I'm still asleep on the couch when the kitchen door slams.

"—all upset, it's for your own good," Mom is saying as I jerk awake and search the ceiling for my location.

"Fuck you, Mom," Geena says. Her voice is exhausted, high-pitched, and wildly angry.

"Don't you *ever* talk to me like that, young lady," Mom says. "You are only sixteen. You are in *my* house. And if *I* say you're not allowed to see him, you're not allowed to see him. And you'll obey me as long as you are under this roof."

Lying here on the sofa, I can hear something I've never noticed before in Mom's voice. I've heard this lecture before. It's usually followed by—

"Dad!" Geena cries. "Are you home, Dad?"

—going to Dad and fomenting an argument between him and Mom in which Mom invariably loses because her crowning argument is "Because I said so," to which Dad will laugh and ruffle his daughter's—whichever daughter it is—hair and say, "Go on, then." And it's all over and things go back to being whatever way they were before. Except that one more ember has been added to the fires of resentment, and one day the fire blazes out of control and the door slams on your heels and you're off to Chicago.

But today, lying here on the sofa—not being able to see Mom's face and not having the lecture directed at me—I hear something I never noticed before.

Fear.

I have a lightbulb moment.

All those screams from my memories click into place under the cartoon incandescent bulb and I know that Mom . . .

. . . Mom is afraid.

I don't know what she's afraid of. Maybe of her daughters running around with unsuitable, unspeakable boys. Maybe of her daughters embarrassing her. Maybe of her daughters leaving her all alone with Dad. Because what could possibly hold them together if both Geena and I are gone?

None of these solutions really fits.

But the desperate sound in her voice every time she confronted Jonz, the tears, the manipulation, even the no-caffeine-after-five thing. It's all about binding us to her and making her world safe. Only we aren't very bindable.

Not even Dad, and he's bound by holy matrimony.

All the doors in the house slam as Geena and Mom go to their respective rooms to duke it out with their pillows. I don't know what to do, so I take the easy route and make coffee—it's before five—and supper.

I'm chopping carrots for vegetable soup when I decide to call Mike. He's in the process of getting The Club ready for the lazy Sunday crowd that will drift in after watching the afternoon's sports. He sounds happy to hear from me.

"I thought you were giving me the cold shoulder," he says. And he sounds like sunshine and fresh air because he's a voice from my life as it is *now*. Or as it was until a few days ago, anyway.

"Did you play 'Watchtower'?" I ask, teasing.

"Almost. Where've you been?"

"Shit Hole, Illinois."

"Hmm. I think I've been there."

We both laugh.

On a whim, I tell him about the lightbulb moment. About the fear in Mom's voice. And I have to tell him about the flour war, too, and the epiphany I had about that.

He laughs. "Pretty interesting," he says.

In the window, I can see my forehead wrinkle. "No, it's important," I say, keeping an eye on the door to the rest of the house. I don't need Mom to find me psychoanalyzing her while standing in her house and using her phone.

"Well, it's good you've figured it out, then," Mike says.

I try hard. Try hard to smile. "It is, isn't it?" I say. All light and cheery.

"Drop by when you get back to Chicago," Mike says. "Maybe that coffee shop will be open this time."

"Right. Take care."

I hang up the phone on the wall unit by the fridge.

"Smile on the outside," Mom says in my head, *"and you'll smile on the inside."*

It was right after Timothy and I had that hand-to-genital exchange. Things had moved pretty quickly to the "what the hell was I thinking?" stage, and I'd made it out of the museum in record time. In other words, I ran. And running along the sidewalk, I didn't even notice the snow. Fat, clumpy flakes of snow. Completely atypical of a Chicago January, when the temperature is too cold for real snow and nothing comes out of the sky but ice and all the snow still on the ground has turned into frozen sand.

I didn't notice the snow. Not until I reached the door of my apartment building—a different apartment building than the one I live in now. I had the beanbag queen of the world for a roommate then. Beanbag chairs, beanbag tables, and some kind of oversized beanbag bed. I'd helped her carry it up five flights of stairs, so I knew it was oversized.

I'm getting sidetracked.

It was snowing, and I was walking—running—away from Timothy and the museum, and outside my apartment building I ran into Jonah. Literally. He grabbed my arm before I could fall on my ass, and I said, "Nice sled."

"I thought you might be up for some late-night sledding," he said, "but Beanbag Girl said you weren't home."

"Yeah."

"Wanna go?"

"Yeah."

I didn't even bother to change. Just turned and followed in his tracks—head down to keep the snow out of my eyes—as we walked around looking for an incline.

"This is good," he said.

I tried to see where we were through the frozen rim of my hat and scarf and snowy eyelashes. I was lost. But it didn't matter. Jonz was with me.

He dropped the sled onto the snow. It wasn't really a sled. More of a plastic toboggan crossed with a mutant saucer. "You'd better sit in front," he said. "I've got thicker gloves."

That makes sense if you understand that the only way to properly steer one of these plastic mutant thingies is by sticking your hand into the snow as you careen down the hill.

"And I'm wearing a skirt," I said. And I thought about Timothy's hand and I felt like throwing up.

"And you're wearing a skirt."

I sat down and held my bag to my chest. Jonz squeezed on behind, his big feet crammed up under my knees.

Then we were off. Weaving through trees and bushes and sliding over hidden bumps and rocks . . . and it felt like the day I drove my first and last car across Hove's city limits. I started laughing and laughing. And I laughed until we hit something . . . and ended up on our backs in the snow.

I looked up at the glitter swirling down through the city lights and the black tree branches. And tears formed in the corners of my eyes. I don't know why.

Jonz sat up. I knew I should sit up so we could slide down the hill again, but then I felt his hand close around mine. And we stayed there— holding hands—until the snow soaked through my coat and turned my back numb. But the whole time, I could feel his skin touch mine through our damp gloves.

I didn't have to try hard to smile.

I hang up the phone on the wall unit by the fridge.

I dump all the vegetables into the garbage—no disposal or recycling in Hove, not even a compost pile—and climb the stairs. I'm not sure where I'm going. My room, maybe. But I end up outside Geena's door. I raise my hand . . . hesitate . . . knock.

"Go away," Geena says. So I turn the knob and walk on in. The house on Maple Street doesn't have any locks. Locks are dangerous in case there's a fire. *"We don't need locks in this house,"* Mom said the day I asked for one. *"There are no secrets in this house."* Which is a nice way to say, "teens don't need privacy," which is a nicer way to say, "if you locked the door, how would I search your room for drugs and condoms?"

So I turn the knob and walk on in.

Geena's lying on her back and staring at the ceiling.

"Hi," I say.

She keeps staring at the ceiling.

"Hey, no need to answer," I say.

"Go away."

"Can't. I drove some stranger's car here and now I'm vehicleless."

"So rent."

"Cough it up," I say, holding out a hand.

She rolls her eyes in my direction. A lazy hound dog keeping track of a fly without moving his head. "Borrow it from Dad."

"I wasn't serious," I say. I sit down on the swivel stool she has in front of her vanity. Twisting back and forth, I look around the room. When I left, it was more nursery than room. I run a finger along the dusty white piece of curlicued furniture with the round mirror that goes with the stool. "Did you pick this out yourself?" I ask.

"Sure," she says. "I picked out everything in this room. I *love* pink and white. Just like you."

"Me?" I ask.

"That's what Mom says."

"I wanted to paint my walls black."

Geena makes a sound between a sob and a snort. Then she starts crying.

I slide off the stool and sit on the bed. I'm new at this—new at thinking of Geena as part of my family—so I lie down on the bed and put my arms around her.

"Go away," she says, but she turns into my shoulder and keeps crying, so I ignore the order.

Her tears soak through the layers of clothing covering my shoulder before she pulls free. I sit up and fumble around until I've found something she can blow her nose on. It's a dirty shirt—one of those little midriff-baring kind—from the floor, but it does the job.

"That's disgusting," she says, holding the shirt away from her.

"It was handy."

She lies back on the pillow and looks at the ceiling again, but without the sullen anger of a few minutes ago. I pull my knees to my chin and just sit on the bed. Waiting.

"Why'd you let them in yesterday?" she asks.

Dylan's family.

"Because they care about you. Because Dylan loves you."

She rubs the shirt under her nose. "Mom says she won't let me see Dylan anymore," she says. "She says she's going to look into bringing him up on statutory rape."

I snort. "He's still a minor."

Geena smiles. "Oh yeah." The smile disappears. "I lost the baby," she whispers.

I nod. "I know."

"Of course you know, you were at the hospital."

"Right. It was a dumb thing to say."

"I didn't really know I *had* a baby," Geena continues, ignoring me. "It was never real, you know? Shouldn't I feel bad or something?"

"You don't?"

She shakes her head back and forth on the pillow.

"Maybe you have to be further along," I say. It sounds weak, but I'm not sure how a person is supposed to feel.

Supposed to feel.

I practically slap myself. This isn't about "supposed to"; this is about reality.

"I don't think I'd feel bad, either," I say.

Geena is frowning at the ceiling, but when my words sink in through whatever thoughts she's having, she looks at me. Surprised.

"I mean," I say, "I've never wanted to have kids, so it may not be relevant at all, but if I were you . . ." I pause. Try to make myself sixteen again. In this house, it isn't hard. Sixteen. Jonz. Morgan. My first cigarette. It feels like a million years ago. It feels like yesterday. "If I were you," I continue, "I would be relieved."

She frowns and starts to open her mouth, but I keep on talking before she has a chance to interrupt.

"I know that probably sounds really nasty, especially since Dylan's family is . . ." I trail off, not sure how to describe them. "I mean, they were excited about having a grandkid and everything. But if it were me, I'd be glad I wasn't going to be a mom. I don't know. I just don't think I've got it in me to *be* a mom, you know? And I had such big plans at sixteen—"

"Like what?" Geena interrupts.

I blink. "Uh . . . to get out of Shit Hole?"

"Ooo, big plans," she says, but she can't help smiling at the saying every high school–age Hovian knows by heart.

"I just wanted to see what life could be like somewhere *else*, somewhere where people don't . . ." I trail off.

"Eat hate three meals a day," she finishes for me.

I wrap my arms tighter around my knees and squeeze. "Yeah."

And it must be a product of all this sisterly togetherness, because I find myself saying something I never thought I'd say. I'm not even sure I believe what I'm saying. "I'm sorry I was such a bitch when you came to Chicago," I say, idiot that I am.

"Yeah, you were," Geena says, which, of course, rides rough over all my warm and fuzzy feelings and helps me remember my dirty bedroom, the trash, the stealing stuff from my roommate, and trying to turn tricks—

"But I wasn't exactly easy," she says.

"Yeah. You practically got me hauled off by the SRS. I'd probably be the only sister in jail for pimping."

She scowls. "I just wanted directions."

"Uh-huh." But I grin. She grins back.

The door opens and Mom walks in. She sees us sitting together on Geena's bed. She stands in the doorway, one hand on the doorknob, one on the door frame, and just looks at us.

"Go away," Geena says.

The skin around Mom's red-rimmed eyes droops, but in her usual voice she says, "I was just going to start supper."

"Fine," Geena says. "Do what you want." Then she rolls over and turns her back to the room.

Mom closes the door.

The exchange makes me uncomfortable. I want to tell Geena to not be such a rude little bitch, but I've been remembering . . .

"Wichita, do you want to set the table?" Mom yelled up the stairs.

Lying on my bed, I turned the pages of the illegal *Cosmo* I'd picked up at the discount store. "How to Get Your Guy Going in Sixty Seconds or LESS!" was the feature article.

"No," I yelled back. I knew the question wasn't about preferences, but my answer was a perfect way to get Mom to lose it.

"Get your butt downstairs right now and set this table."

"You asked me if I wanted to," I yelled back. "I don't." I slipped the *Cosmo* under my pillow. But not soon enough.

Mom grabbed it and pulled it out again. "What is *this*?"

"A magazine. Are you blind or something?"

• • •

. . . I've been remembering what a rude little bitch I was—on purpose—so what's the point of pointing it out to Geena?

"I'd better go help her with supper," I say.

"Why bother?" Geena asks. "It's not *our* idea to eat together. No one else does it."

I think about Dylan's family. She must see what I'm thinking because she says, "You think they'd all fit around one table?"

"Right."

I shut the door behind me and go downstairs to the kitchen.

Chapter 20

People say that food brings a family together. I don't know who these people are, but I'd like to meet one of them. I'd like to know the name of *one* person who actually let that pithy saying out of his or her mouth. Because if I knew that person's name, I could go on the Internet, track him or her down, and bring them to the kitchen on Maple Street.

I'd like to do that. I really would. Because then this mysterious people person would find some other pithy saying to spout and leave the food in peace.

"Why are all these carrots in the garbage?" Mom asks as I walk into the kitchen.

"They were bad," I say.

She reaches in—yucky—and pulls out one of the half-chopped carrots. She sniffs it. "It looks fine to me."

I bite my tongue. I want to say, *"Then why don't you wash it off and cook it?"* but that sounds a little too sixteen-year-old for me. I'm an adult twenty-eight now. Okay, forget the adult part. I'm twenty-eight now. I don't live here anymore. I can deal with this.

"I meant they were naughty," I say.

No, no, no, no. That is *not* how to deal with this.

Mom frowns.

"I was upset," I say, jumping in before she can get started on whether or not this is a good time for puns, "about . . . everything. I got angry and I threw them away. I shouldn't have done that."

She looks at me out of those red-rimmed eyes, then gently returns the garbage can to its place under the sink. "You can waste the food when you buy it," she says.

"I know," I say, thinking about Geena and Dylan buying pizza and letting my alternate, full-moon Tuesday groceries rot in the fridge. "I know. I'm sorry."

She nods. "What were you fixing?"

I can't remember.

"Vegetable soup," I lie, just as I remember it's not a lie.

"That sounds good. Only we'll have to make do without the carrots." She sighs. As if somehow doing without carrots is like trying to make do without oxygen. She hands me a five-pound sack of potatoes. "You can peel these."

"We need all of them? There's only four of us."

She sighs again. "We don't have any carrots."

"Oh." I look at the bag. Dirty, eye-filled potatoes look back. "Do I have to peel them? Won't that just waste vitamins or something?"

"Not if you peel them correctly."

I close my eyes. The potatoes are howling with laughter.

"You can clean them in the laundry room sink," Mom says as she begins laying out a row of well-behaved, well-scrubbed stalks of celery on the cutting board.

"Maybe we should just have spaghetti," I say, looking at the celery stalks and having fond memories of cooking supper the other night when I thought I'd be gone forty hours ago.

"We already had spaghetti this week. Variety is good nutrition." She decapitates the unsuspecting celery. "You'd better hurry or the potatoes won't be done in time for supper."

Scrubbing the laughing potatoes under a frigid stream of water—the laundry room sink is missing a hot water tap—I think up vile tortures for the person who said food could bring a family together. The person was probably a man. Someone who showed up at the table and never participated in the process. I think up vile tortures because I believed him, and made the mistake of coming downstairs and voluntarily submitting myself to the agony of scrubbing and—worse—peeling potatoes.

My hands are numb from the water and I'm on the third potato before I notice the pink smears. The paring knife peeled my thumb, and I never felt a thing. I look at the blood welling up from the place where the white corkscrew scar used to be and—

I miss Jonz.

Blood drips onto the potatoes.

"Honey?" Mom says, shaking me out of my trance. "Oh, dear Lord." She's seen my thumb.

"I cut myself," I say. "Pretty dumb of me."

But I don't mean my thumb.

I'm thinking about the scalpel and the office and cutting off half of myself. Because Jonz and I aren't joined anymore and Monday night is "D-Day" and he's going to be with Janet. And there's no reason he should think about me because I told him . . .

I want away from you.

The gasp starts in my chest, but I swallow it.

Mom grabs my hand and holds it under the water until the bleeding stops. She inspects the cut. "We should take you in and have this stitched."

"No," I say. "It's all right."

I want away from you.

I deserve to have the mark of family removed from me.

"It's all right," I say again. "I'll put a Band-Aid on it and it will be all right."

It's a dirty lie.

"You'll have a scar," she says.

I shrug.

She looks down at the potatoes. "And you've ruined—" She cuts off the sentence before she can say, *"You've ruined the potatoes by bleeding all over them."* "I'll find a Band-Aid," she says instead.

By the time she comes back, I can feel my thumb stinging. I make a butterfly bandage by clipping the Band-Aid, then pull the skin of my thumb together.

"That won't work," she says.

"Probably not."

"I'm sorry."

"It's okay."

"No," she says, "I'm sorry I sent you in here by yourself. We don't really need all those potatoes, and I almost never peel them anymore. Unless we have mashed ones, that is. Your father doesn't like the peels in his mashed potatoes, although sometimes I think it adds texture and isn't really all that bad."

We stare at each other.

"To hell with dinner," she says. "Let's have some coffee and Sandies."

"What the hell were you thinking—" Dad said as he slammed the back door shut.

I looked up from my homework. I was sitting at the kitchen table, puzzling through the latest mathematical torture—fractions, I think—and the sun had almost disappeared.

"They were out of Sandies," Mom said. She set her purse down on the other end of the table.

"—lying on the floor like a two-year-old, kicking and screaming because of some *cookies!*" Dad continues.

"Brad—"

"And they called me at *work*. Called me to come get you at *work*. Everybody knows."

"I'm having a baby, Brad."

"Goddammit, Maggie, this isn't the time to kid around. . . ." He trailed off. "You're serious."

She nodded, her finger tracing patterns on the blue vinyl of her purse.

"Well, fuck me," Dad said.

Mom frowned. "Don't talk like that."

"I'll talk any way I damn well please."

I shrank into my math book, wished the printed numbers would grab me and pull me in.

Mom went to the sink and filled the teakettle.

"What are you doing?" Dad asked.

"Making something hot to drink."

"I mean about the baby."

The water flowed over the edge of the teakettle's top and ran down the drain.

"Never mind," he said. The back door slammed again. This time as Dad went out.

I tried to keep solving word problems about sale prices on a fictional pair of shoes while pretending nothing unusual had happened. Mom sat at the other end of the table and ate an entire bag of Oreos—each cookie carefully dipped in a cup of instant decaf coffee.

Later that night, I heard her throwing up in the bathroom down the hall.

Dad never came home.

Mom and I stare at each other.

"To hell with dinner," she says. "Let's have some coffee and Sandies."

Sitting beside her at the table, I wonder if I owe the nameless person with his food quote an apology. Except Mom isn't talking. But I guess the saying only promised togetherness, not conversation.

Mom dips and eats.

I wrap my fingers around the hot mug in front of me and try not to breathe in the nauseating scent of pecans.

"Why Pecan Sandies?" I ask when the coffee in my mug has turned lukewarm.

"Grandma was allergic to nuts."

I wait for further explanation, but none comes.

"What happened to all those colored bottles Grandma had?" I'm not sure why I'm asking. Maybe because the gray evening light seems even more gray after it pushes its way through the dusty glass of the kitchen window.

"Your father's been gone all day," Mom says. "He never called to see if Geena got home all right."

"Maybe he thought you would call him," I say, forgetting it's Sunday. Forgetting Dad's cell is in his briefcase in the living room. Forgetting Dolores.

She frowns at me. Dunks another Sandie into her decaf coffee. "I think they're in the attic."

So the bottles and the little house were real. I can take the colored memories of playing on rainbowed hardwood floors and add them to my cigar box. What did I play with? I'm digging into my memory treasury when Mom stands up to get another cup of coffee and distracts me.

"And the bottles weren't your grandma's," she says. "They were mine."

I open my mouth, but she interrupts me.

"Oh, look. Your father's home."

"How's Geena?" Dad asks as he opens the door.

Mom adds water to the teakettle, puts it on the stove, then occupies herself by spooning instant coffee into her cup.

The silence stretches.

"She's okay," I say into the void. "She's upstairs. Sleeping."

He nods, then turns to Mom. "Why didn't you call me?"

"And where would I reach you?" she asks.

Silence.

The teakettle whistles.

Dad reaches out and shakes her shoulder. "Maggie? You okay?"

She gives him a puzzled look. "Oh, were you at work today? When you didn't call, I just assumed . . ." And she trails off in mock puzzlement. Then she smiles. "Well, now I know, don't I? Are you hungry?"

He lets go of her shoulder, as if she's just turned into a stranger. As if he were out searching for a lost woman in Chicago. Grabbing strangers and pulling them around, looking for a familiar face.

"No," he says. "I ate out." *With someone else.*

"Oh, good," Mom says, smiling. "Because we didn't make you any food."

His face wrinkles up into a knot, then he throws his coat onto the table and goes into the living room to watch TV.

Mom pushes the coat onto the floor before she sits down with a fresh cup of coffee. Picking up the cookie bag, she gropes around inside the crackling package for the last of the Sandies. "You can have those bottles," she says to me. "If you want them."

Ch ap te r 21

I taught Jonz to ride a bike on the late June afternoon of my eighth birthday. I'd gotten a bicycle—a shiny blue one—and Dad had instilled the rudimentary principles of riding into my head during an afternoon when the cable went on the fritz and he couldn't watch preseason football. After the cable miraculously fixed itself, he went back into the house even though I begged him to stay outside with me.

He pretended not to hear.

Determined, I kept fighting the bike until it was bruised and I was bloody. Mom came out and tried to get me to quit, but I screamed and pounded my fists on the sidewalk. I guess she recognized enough of herself to leave me to it. After a nasty collision with the mailbox, I watched the stars twirling around in the sky and listened to Mom's voice seeping out of the living room, where she was talking at Dad.

"You might as well not even exist," she said.

Lying there, knees bleeding and gravel pressing into my elbows, I knew I would ride that bike if it killed me.

Because I didn't want Mom and Dad to fight anymore.

I only fell down once during the half-mile ride to Jonah's house. I found him sitting on his front steps. He was digging at the underside of the stair railing with his knife—cutting unhappy marks into the same stick of wood caressed by people entering and leaving the house. Through the curtains, I could hear a woman's voice rising and falling. A human train whistle of warning.

"Look at me!" I said to Jonz as I pedaled up the sidewalk, still basking in a triumphal haze.

He closed the knife and grinned. "You got it!"

Having my own bicycle had been the sole dream of glory in my soon-to-be-eight mind. Mom had dropped a hint after she'd found me staring at the row of gleaming metal during a trip to Wal-Mart. *"Be good and you just might get one."*

I'd let her make me wear pink four Sundays in a row.

"Wanna try it?" I asked, but Jonz shook his head.

Disappointment flared in my stomach. "You don't like it?"

"I don't know how," he said.

"I can teach you."

He looked at my knees. "Are you sure?"

But, making up my own rudimentary principles, I got him onto the bike. He promptly fell over. "I did that, too," I said, squatting down beside him and feeling a tiny thrill of satisfaction that even the great Jonz fell over the first time.

"No need to be so happy about it," he said. And it was the last fall he took.

We were trying a wobbly double—both of us on the long seat—when Zeke, Jonah's brother, came out onto the porch. "Hey, Jonz," he called. "Come here."

"In a minute."

"Now."

We wobbled our way up the sidewalk, and Jonz hopped off. "What?" he asked.

"Dad's gone," Zeke said, all the wisdom of being ten rather than eight oozing out of his voice.

"So?"

"He's *gone*," he said again, emphasizing the word. "He's not coming back."

I stared at him. I'd only met Jonah's dad once—that long-ago day in first grade. He was always "gone." But this "gone" seemed more permanent than the usual "gone," and that could only mean . . .

"He's *dead?*" I whispered.

Zeke snorted. "Yeah, right. Dummy."

Jonah turned pale. "You're lying."

His brother shrugged and went back into the house.

"You're *lying*," Jonah said again, running after Zeke.

I crept through the door, following Jonah. I'd been in the house before, but usually we roamed the fields out back with Shep in tow. The house had too many secrets. It hid them in the floorboards and under the stairs. Just inside the door, Shep lay on the floor, his lips spread out in a doggy sulk. I plopped down beside him and scratched his ears. His tail didn't thump. On the other side of the room, baby Craig screamed out his frustration from behind the playpen's walls.

Jonah's mother sat on the couch in the living room. She was small and pretty, not like my mom, who had to wear housedresses to cover the rolls around her waist. She hugged Jonz, but he pulled away, angry. "It's *your* fault," he said. "Your fault."

His mother stood up and walked away.

"Get a clue, stupid," Jonz' older sister, Caro, said. "Dad doesn't want any of us. Not even you."

Jonz jumped up and pushed Caro. She fell back into a chair. He ran past me and out the door. I got up to follow him. When I looked back at Caro, she had a pillow over her face and her shoulders shook.

I rode my bike all over town.

I never found Jonah.

When I got home, Mom was livid. I was late for supper and she'd been worried I'd gone and killed myself on "that bike."

"I was looking for Jonah—" I began.

"Not again—" Mom said.

"—because he ran off after finding out his dad died."

"If I've told you . . ." Mom's voice faded away.

I stared at her. Then at Dad. He was watching Mom, and a twitch worked in the corner of his mouth.

"He didn't die," Dad said. "He left town."

Mom gripped the edge of the table in her hands. I sat down in front of my bowl of cold vegetable soup, picked up my spoon, and hoped no one would remember I was late if I ate and kept quiet.

"And he didn't take anyone with him," Dad said.

How did he know that? A spoonful of soup held between my mouth and the bowl, I started to ask, but Dad wasn't paying any attention to me.

"Poor little Magpie Bird," he said.

Something squeezes my lungs together and I wake up gasping. As if I'd been holding my breath in my sleep. I actually make a kind of whining scream as the air slides into my lungs.

Poor little Magpie Bird.

What the hell?

I haven't thought about the day Jonah's dad left since . . . since the day of his mother's funeral. We were standing around in the funeral parlor, and some woman whispered something about an ex-husband. And the whisper whirled me back in time and I remembered sitting next to Shep and the fear and rage on Jonz' face. I carefully kept Jonz away from the woman who'd been whispering. Not because I didn't think he could handle questions about his dad fifteen or so years later, but because if someone asked he'd have to say, "I don't know where my father is." And no one should have to say that at their mother's funeral.

But even at the funeral, I didn't take the bicycle memory of hunting for Jonz to the vegetable-soup conclusion.

Lying on the couch in the dark, I watch the frost creep up the moonlit living room window. When the heater comes on, the frost will melt and puddle on the sill, threatening to drip off the edge and onto the carpet if someone doesn't mop it up with a dish towel.

Poor little Magpie Bird.

Something nags.

I roll onto my side, but I slept too much today and my stomach is growling.

And looking at the window makes me think about the bottles Mom said I could have. For some reason, it's important to me to go upstairs and get those bottles and carry them back to my apartment and the minuscule window over the sink. India will like them.

Pulling on a pair of sweats, I creep up the stairs and down the hall to the door leading up the stairs to the attic. When Hove was first building houses, the upscale ones added attics. Crawl spaces, really. You can't stand up in one. So unless you want to walk around bent at a ninety-degree angle, you shuffle along on your butt. Scooting along, I reach up for the light string and turn on the bare bulb attached to one of the roof beams. It's cold up here. Cold enough to see my breath. I tuck my hands into my armpits and look around at the boxes lining the attic walls.

It isn't the kind of attic children have fun in. There are no ancient pirate trunks, coat trees, shadowy dress forms, or even old lamps. One wall has boxes marked GEENA'S BABY CLOTHES, GEENA'S OLD TOYS, and GEENA'S FIRST PROM DRESS. There are no boxes marked WICHITA. All my stuff went to Goodwill after I left for Chicago. I can see the bare spots where the boxes used to sit.

A tiny prick of pain.

But my memories are in my head. Where they belong.

I'm not sure which box would have the bottles, but I start rummaging at random. Quietly rummaging. I don't want to wake anyone up.

I find the bottles underneath a yellow-checked dress. The dress is early-seventies vintage. Back when clothes were shapeless and unattractive. It has a thin yellow ribbon that ties in a bow under the boobs. An empire waist. Tiny, tight cap sleeves kept poofy with elastic. And white platform shoes, which would be in again if they weren't uglier than the retro versions.

The shoes have been tossed in on top of the bottles. I pick them up and set them aside. Something slides around and pokes out one open toe. I almost ignore it, but it's a picture. Which is strange, because Mom is a photograph bloodhound. She saves every picture ever developed in the bank of photo albums downstairs.

I pull the picture free of the shoe. It's one of those square three-by-threes where the colors are fading to red. On the left is Mom—looking like Geena—in the yellow-checked dress. From the flowers in her hair, I'd say it's a prom picture. She's standing next to a boy whose face is obscured by a big lipstick print of a kiss. I hold the picture up to the light.

And let it drop.

It's Jonz.

No, you idiot.

I pick up the picture. Not Jonz. The eyes aren't right. And the face is softer. Plus, he's standing next to my mom, and even if she's got the extra three inches from the platform shoes . . . well, he's shorter than Jonz.

Poor little Magpie Bird.

Ah, Jesus.

Lightbulb moment.

Some lightbulb moments are night-light-sized, and some are more like the stadium lights that all the astronomers complain about because they brighten the sky and ruin the stargazing. This lightbulb moment shines too hard and cold on too many things in my life.

I'm sitting in a dusty crawl space storage area, my breath blowing cold and visible on a picture.

And I'm standing on a bleeding leg between my mother and Jonz. *"This is all your fault."*

And I'm watching an unfamiliar smile on my mother's face as she dances, eyes closed, on an impromptu living room dance floor. *"What are you trying to do, Maggie? Don't play that game with me."*

And I'm waiting for my father to decide if Jonah and I can be friends. *"What's the matter, Maggie? You afraid she'll turn out just like you?"*

And I'm watching the malicious light in the nurse's eyes. *"Just like old times, huh?"*

"Poor little Magpie Bird."

"He left town. And he didn't take anyone with him."

"Poor little Magpie Bird."

And I'm sitting on a bed with damp hair falling down my back, and Jonz is asking me if we're destined to repeat the mistakes of our parents.

Did Jonz know about my mother and his father? Or—I look down at the picture—was this just some prom date thing? A "Filthy Jeff with flowers in your hair" kind of date.

No.

The lightbulb moment is too clear, too bright, too illuminating.

I shiver. And the shiver covers the sound of the door opening.

I hear the footsteps on the stairs at the same time as someone snatches the picture out of my hand.

"Where did you find this?" Mom asks. Hisses. Or whispers. Maybe she just doesn't want to wake anyone up either.

I point to the box.

And as I point, I realize that there are only four things in this box that is large enough to hold a hundred cigar boxes. There's a dress, a pair of shoes, a picture, and a row of colored bottles.

"Oh, Mom," I say. And I start crying.

It's the tiny number. Only four. And four seems so pathetic and too small to make up the good parts of someone's life. Only four things. Two plus two. My God, you can't even remember memories from when you were four.

"What are you crying about?" she whispers.

"Nothing," I say, rubbing a hand under my running nose. "No, too *little* something."

She doesn't ask what I mean. "Come downstairs," she says. "You're freezing."

I shake my head. "I want the bottles."

"Did I say you could have them?" she asks, surprised.

"Yes, but I don't want them. For me, I mean."

She holds the dress and shoes to her chest. The picture is gone, but it's still there in both our minds, even if it's hidden in one of the square patch pockets on the outside of her housecoat. "What will I do with these?" she asks.

I pull down a little box filled with GEENA'S BABY CLOTHES. I open the tape holding the flaps shut and dump the baby stuff out onto the floor. "Here," I say, handing Mom the box.

She folds the yellow-checked dress and puts it into the box, on top of the white shoes. I don't ask if the picture is in the box; I just close the cardboard flaps and set it back on top of the stack.

"I should take these to Goodwill," Mom says, looking down at the pile of baby bibs and socks. "I don't know why I keep them."

I do, but it seems too exhausting and useless to say, *"You keep them to hurt me, Mom. Hurt me for leaving you behind. For leaving like you should have done."*

We both know that already.

"Come downstairs," she says again. And juggling the box of colored bottles, I follow her down the attic stairs, down the main stairs, and into the kitchen, where the dawn tinges the dusty window with gray light.

"I hate you!" I screamed into the gray dawn. Then I let the screen door slam behind me as I ran down the sidewalk, past the bird feeders, and through the gate in the picket fence—it had a new coat of white paint— to the car that had cost me half my Burger King savings.

"Come back here," Mom yelled from the front porch. "Where do you think you're going?"

I didn't answer. I threw my bag—just a small bag, only large enough to hold the necessary things like pictures and journals and Pooky-Bear and my acceptance letter to the University of Chicago. I threw my bag into the back seat and started the engine. Mom reached the open gate in time to see me pull away from the curb.

My hands shook as I drove the familiar streets along the railroad tracks. I pulled up in front of Jonah's house and left the motor running because I didn't know if it would start again. I didn't care if it died a mile outside of Hove, but I couldn't bear it if it died before I'd crossed that invisible line.

I threw a handful of gravel at Jonz' window. Thirty seconds later, he opened the front door and stepped out, wearing nothing but a pair of sweats in the chill gray wind of my last June morning in Hove. He leaned his crossed arms on the porch railing and grinned at me.

"Is that piece of shit fouling our air yours?" he asked.

I started laughing. "Yeah."

"The oil goes in the little hole under the hood," he said, miming the action. "You only put gasoline into the gas tank. It's not a two-stroke lawn mower."

"Are you coming?" I asked.

"Where?"

"Chicago. Or to wherever the Lawn-Boy decides to break down."

"Now?"

I nodded. Then laughed again.

"Hang on." He opened the door and went back into the silent, sleeping house.

Five minutes later he was throwing a bag beside mine on the back seat.

And I knew how it felt to stand in front of a freight train and stretch out your arms to embrace the world and life and death and whatever might smack you in the chest. Or not.

Jonz called his family from a gas station seventy-five miles up the road.

I never called mine.

Juggling the box of colored bottles, I follow Mom down the attic stairs, down the main stairs, and into the kitchen, where the dawn tinges the dusty window with gray light.

"I'll make some coffee," she says.

I set the box onto the table and pull out the bottles. Safe under the prom dress, they're as clean as when they were put away. I don't bother washing them, just line them up on the upper edge of the double-hung kitchen window. On cue, the morning sun slides its fingers through the rainbow glass. Turning around, I see my mother leaning against the counter that runs along the wall opposite the window. The colors surround her like the blessing candles around the statue of the Virgin Mary.

"You had a miscarriage, didn't you?" I say. But it's not really a question. "And Jared LiaKos was the father."

She drops her head and the red, blue, gold, and green play across the gray hair mixed with brown. "I was sixteen," she says.

I nod.

"Afterward, Mama told me I wasn't allowed to see him anymore. She locked me in my room for three days. Then she sent me to live with her sister in Springfield for the rest of the summer."

I wait for the inevitable story of rejection. How she came back to Hove, tried to contact Jared, only he had a new girl, prettier and with a thinner waist. The story doesn't come.

"What happened?" I ask.

She smiles an empty smile. "I obeyed my mother. Jared tried to talk to me, but I told him I didn't want to see him anymore."

I want away from you.

Ah, Jesus.

"Are you all right?" Mom asks.

"We repeat the mistakes of our parents," I whisper into the rainbow dawn.

Chapter 22

Learning from the past is tricky. Not only do you need historical knowledge, you also have to recognize history when it shows up in the present. But what happens when the past refuses to cough up the details?

Did Jonz know about Maggie and Jared? Imagining him knowing and never telling me, keeping secrets from me, I feel my brain cringe away from . . . But it doesn't matter. Maybe he tried to tell me that rainy afternoon. Maybe he only guessed. Maybe the lightbulb never even went off.

It doesn't matter.

"I have to go back to Chicago," I say into the rainbow dawn.

"Now?" Mom asks.

I'm pulling on my boots and throwing socks and sweats into my bag. "Yes."

And I don't care about D-Day and Janet and whether or not I have the right to beg forgiveness. I don't care if I can't sew the Siamese twins back together. Maybe they shouldn't be sewn back together. But I have to go home.

Home to my family.

I open the door and I'm halfway down the sidewalk when I realize the Lawn-Boy isn't out there by the curb and I don't even have a car and it's a long, cold walk to the rental.

And I didn't say good-bye.

Mom is standing just inside the storm door, her arms wrapped around her waist and the lipstick-smeared picture in her pocket.

I open the door and kiss her on the cheek. "Dylan loves her," I say. "They'll make mistakes. Let them. He loves her. Don't drive them apart. Or away."

She frowns a little, but she nods.

And turning around, I step off the porch and I walk away from the house on Maple Street. The house on Maple Street, where a man never felt good enough and took out his bitterness on a woman who never had the courage to admit to herself that she couldn't live a life based on "supposed to." And like a bunch of starlings, they pecked and screamed and fought.

But unlike a bunch of starlings, they never looked out for each other.

My boots crunch in the frozen snow.

Above me, the sun sends a shaft of light singing down the electrical lines.

"You're soaked," Jonz said after he helped me up from the snow. He had reached down for the sled, and in the process his cheek had brushed the back of my shoulder. He grabbed my shoulders and turned my back to the light. "Your coat's all wet."

"I'm okay," I said, but I was already shivering.

He looked up into the swirling snow. Whether he was looking for the points of the compass or patience, I don't know. And at the time I was shivering too hard to care.

"Come on," he said, reaching down for my hand.

"My bag."

He picked it up and swung it over his shoulder.

"You're kind of an idiot," he said as he helped me over the wrought-iron fence that separated the hill from the path beyond it. "If it weren't for me, you'd freeze to death in a snowbank."

"If it weren't for you," I said through rattling teeth, "I'd be snuggled up on my couch with some hot chocolate, not sledding at midnight."

"It's always my fault, isn't it?" His smile flashed in the glow of the streetlight.

"Of course." My feet were sluggish in the snow.

"I bet I can carry you for a city block," he said when we reached the sidewalk again.

I shook my head.

His eyebrows disappeared into his hair. "No?"

"No." It took effort to talk.

"Piggyback," he said. Then he tossed the sled into the nearest Dumpster.

I tried to protest the loss of the sled, but that would have taken too much effort.

"Up here," he said, helping me onto a cement step. Then he turned his back to me. I stared at it.

"—stupid," I managed through my teeth.

"Get on."

And I heard something in his voice I hadn't heard since that time when I fell through the bleachers and bled all over the kitchen floor.

"You just think I'll win," he said.

"Screw you," I mumbled, and I put my arms over his shoulders and wrapped my legs around his waist.

He carried me all the way to his apartment door.

I'm shivering by the time I reach Scaletti Rentals. Cars line the lot, shrouded in holland covers of snow. There's light and human motion in the office, so I pound my frozen fist on the glass door. The CLOSED sign swings from side to side, tapping the glass and keeping time.

A head pokes out of the office. A finger points at the sign. I shrug and hold up my hands in silent appeal. The head pokes out farther. Eyes peer at me from behind thick, fashionable glasses. Underneath the glasses, a mouth twists in disgust.

"We're *closed*," he says when he opens the door. He bangs on the sign for emphasis.

"Hi, Jeff," I say, being careful to use the tone and accent I had eleven years ago, before Chicago wiped the plains out of me.

He keeps thumping on the sign, but he's looking at me and searching his memories—

"Wichita?"

And then he blushes. Probably because he's remembered the year or two he spent camped out in front of my locker after the sophomore dance. The year or two I spent finding ingenious ways to avoid him. Like climbing in the window of the girls' restroom.

"I really need to rent a car," I say, helping us both over this red-faced moment.

"We open in an—",

"I need one now. For a one-way to Chicago."

He frowns. "But—"

I'm nearly to the point of begging when a car pulls up in front of the office. We turn around. Well, I turn around since Filthy . . . since *Jeff*, I mean, is already facing that direction. The car is one of those German sports car thingies. I can never keep them straight. BMW, Porsche, something like that. And the woman getting out of the car is one of those interchangeable svelte creatures that seem to go *with* German sports cars.

Only it's Morgan.

The Morgan of green Volvo fame.

Of rocking the green Volvo with Jonz fame.

For the first time, I acknowledge that the little stab in my chest has nothing to do with my friend being an idiot.

"Hi, honey," she says, giving Jeff a kiss on the cheek. She's holding a bag from the local pastry shop and a cup carrier with two cups of coffee. "They didn't have unglazed this morning, so I just got the chocolate frosted."

Then she looks at me. Looks at my hair, my clothes, my boots. Something about me tells her I'm not from here, and yet I'm obviously here and people don't stop by Hove without a reason.

She frowns. "Don't I know you?"

"High school," I say, biting my wicked tongue before it can say, *"Hey, remember Jonah LiaKos?"*

Just to see if she'd jump.

She probably wouldn't even remember.

"And?" she asks.

"And I'd like to rent a car," I say.

"Well, rent her a car, Jeff. It's cold out here." And she slips through the door and goes into the office.

Jeff smiles and shrugs. "Come on in," he says. "I didn't mean to be rude, but you caught me by surprise."

I smile and try not to sneak a peek at his ears to see if he's started using Q-tips since I saw him last. "It's a bit of a—" I start to say "emergency," but that might cause questions I'm not comfortable answering with Morgan setting out the coffee and doughnuts. "It's a bit of a rush," I say instead. I look over at Morgan. Our eyes meet and we smile at each other. The friend and the one-night-stand. "I hope I'm not interrupting your breakfast."

Morgan waves a dismissive hand and smiles. "It's all right."

This from the girl who said, *"Watch it, bitch,"* if you got within three feet of her leather jacket. If I thought it were possible, I would say that Morgan has given Jeff some spine, and Jeff has given Morgan some heart. But I'm having a hard enough time putting the two of them together. I mean, how did they meet? Romantically, that is. Did they go out on a date? Get drunk and get over the no-bath, earwax thing through an alcohol haze? Or did Jeff clean up first?

"Here you go," Jeff says, sliding a piece of paper across the counter. With one nicely manicured finger, he taps the line I'm supposed to sign. "Complimentary upgrade for being an old friend."

Surprised, I look up. He smiles at me. "Thank you," I say.

"No, thank you." And it's a thank-you for going to the dance, keeping him out of the punch, and the damp kiss on the doorstep.

"You're welcome," I say.

"Would you like a doughnut?" Morgan asks.

But the whole "Morgan as domestic goddess" thing is just too strange for me, so I smile and shake my head. "No, thanks. I have to get going."

Tossing my bag into the passenger seat, I'm almost surprised the happy couple isn't watching me through the front glass and waving me off.

I start to turn onto the road that will take me to the freeway and to Chicago, but I remember one last thing I have to do.

"I'm sorry I'm such a pain in the ass," I said to Jonz. I was sitting on his couch, warm from a hot shower and wrapped in one of his old flannel shirts and an old afghan he'd bought at a thrift shop.

He handed me a cup of instant chicken noodle soup from his microwave. "It keeps me from getting lazy," he said.

I squinted at him through the steam.

"Pain in the ass?" he said, making a circular "do I really have to explain this?" motion with his hand. "Can't sit down?"

"Oh. Got it." I grinned over the mug. It was the mate of the one I had—have—in my apartment. Jonz had made the pair during a ceramics class in college. The mugs were thin, delicate, and had the wrinkled face of a tree spirit squeezed into the sides. We were both broke the Christmas after the ceramics class, and he had given me one of the cups. I gave him a collection of my poems. I still think I got the better end of the deal.

Jonz pulled off his sweaty shirt. Even now, I weigh more than I look, and he had carried me a long way. It took me a foggy, chicken-soup minute to realize what was missing.

"Where's the key?" I asked.

The key. We'd found it among the roots of the oak tree while digging roads. It was one of those old skeleton-type keys, only it was small—like the key to a jewelry box. Jonz had worn it around his neck for so long, it was practically a part of him.

Now it was gone.

He shrugged into a dry shirt. "I think it's still in the cigar box," he said.

I nodded.

I start to turn onto the road that will take me to the freeway and to Chicago, but I remember one last thing I have to do. Because I've just remembered the other time I saw Jonz without the key.

The morning we left for Chicago.

Which means the cigar box is still in Hove.

Driving beside the railroad tracks, I turn the heater on high and try to get warm.

The house Jonah grew up in still exists. Barely. His mother moved into a hospice when cancer moved into her body. I think Caro and her husband might have rented the place out for a while, but the name LIAKOS is still visible on the mailbox. After a while, even Caro couldn't deal with the responsibility of keeping things up long-distance. And the house sat empty. I'm not sure why an empty house falls apart so quickly after the door is closed for the last time. Maybe the wooden beams crack and disintegrate from the pain of living all alone.

I park the car where I parked the Lawn-Boy eleven years ago. But this time I shut off the engine. If the car refuses to start, Jeff and Morgan are a phone call away. And since it's their car, they'll have to send someone to give me a jump. I'm guaranteed a four-wheel trip to Chicago.

The porch stairs creak under my boots, and my hand caresses the railing notched twenty years ago by an angry child's knife. I can feel the gouges under my fingertips. The bank owns the house now. I'm trespassing. And the house is dangerous. No one can live here until it's brought up to code or demolished.

At least that's what the sign on the door says. I ignore it and reach up high and into the peeling gingerbread frame of the porch. The spare key still hangs from a discreet nail. The spare key still fits the lock on the door. You'd think someone might have changed the locks, but it doesn't surprise me to find things unchanged. Things never change in Hove.

Swollen into its frame by damp and rot, the door refuses to open until I introduce it to my shoulder. The house moans and creaks as I intrude on its dreams. I can still smell the secrets under the stairs and buried beneath the rippling floorboards. I swallow, and my throat is dry. I promise myself a cup of rest-stop coffee if I can ignore the secrets.

The stairs seem solid enough, but I test each step on the way up to Jonah's room. I know the way, but things feel wrong without the faded rugs in the hall and glossy five-by-seven school pictures on the wall. The door to Jonz' room is closed. I push it open and feel the floor shift.

No.

It's just my memories that shift.

The wallpaper is the same faded stripe, but the furniture is gone. Only a darker line along the wall where the bed used to be. Where we sat and Jonz asked me if we made the mistakes of our parents—

Oh, God. I hope not.

—and my hair hung damp.

A lighter spot where the dresser stood. I kneel down in front of that spot and push on a part of the wooden trim between the floor and the wall. Nothing happens. I push harder. Maybe this isn't the right place? But something groans a little, and cracks appear. No, the wall is just swollen. Like the door.

I dig my fingernails in between the faded paper and the trim and pull. A piece of the trim pops away. And like those paperbacks that come in a cardboard slipcover, I know I'll never get the piece back in.

On my hands and knees, I lay my cheek on the floor and I reach into the dark hole—bravely ignoring the skittering noises I'm sure I hear, although it might just be my imagination—and pull out a cardboard box.

The cigar box.

And for the first time this morning, I feel like I'm trespassing.

But I just want to see if the key . . .

It's there. On top.

On top of so many things. I was right. I would never find the black puppy hairs and whisker in this jumble of memories. I might not even find a photograph if someone left one behind.

I shut the box.

Out on the freeway, drivers turn on their headlights as we negotiate a concrete river of fog.

Chapter 23

Despite the fog and snow, I make it to Chicago by late afternoon. Which means Jonah is at the museum. Assuming he hasn't made good on his threat to leave. I swallow my pride and park the car within walking distance of the old building. I rented the car for a full day, so I might as well get my money's worth before I have to turn it in. I'm scared of leaving the cigar box all alone on the front seat where it might get stolen, so I carry it with me.

The first person I run into is Timothy.

"About time you showed up," he says. "Where the hell have you been?"

"Family situation," I say. "Remember?"

And this is why I haven't been losing my mind thinking about job safety. A little surprised that Janet seemed to know so much about my employment opportunities, but still not worried much beyond the knowledge that the unemployment line is a nasty line to stand in.

Besides, if push came to shove, I could always blackmail Timothy into giving me back my job. He is my boss, after all, so whatever we did was probably illegal. Assuming, of course, that he *remembers* the hand-to-genital exchange. It was a while ago. And Timothy can't remember his last name half the time.

"'Family situation'?" Timothy asks. "What kind of an excuse is that?"

"Is Jonz here?" I ask.

"How the hell would I know?" He starts to stomp off, then comes back. "I need that grant proposal tomorrow," he says.

"No, you don't."

He glares at me.

"It's not due until *next* month."

"Oh." His mouth works, then he points a commanding finger at my office door. "Well, get to work."

"Tomorrow," I say.

"Fine. Tomorrow, then. What's that?" he asks, pointing at the cigar box.

"Nothing. Is Jonz here?"

"How the hell would I know?"

"See you tomorrow," I say to his retreating back.

He waves a hand over his head.

I walk down the hall to the coffee room. But it's empty. Not even the semipermanent Kenny fixture is around. Stepping back out into the hall, I carefully check to the left and right. I don't want to admit it to myself, but I'm afraid of running into Janet. I'm afraid I'll stoop to doing something low.

Like spitting.

"D-Day is Monday."

The bitch.

I duck into the bathroom to give myself time to think. Dorothy comes out of one of the stalls, and gives me an unpleasant twirl of déjà vu.

"Hi," I say. "How are you feeling?"

She turns around and goes back into the stall.

"Do you know if Jonah's here?" I ask when I think it might be safe to ask questions.

"It's Monday," she says. "I don't even know why *I'm* here."

"Don't remind me," I say. "I was trying to forget about D-Day."

Her eyebrows meeting over her nose, Dorothy peers out of the stall. "You should see your doctor," she says, all motherly concern. "Pregnancy doesn't have to—"

"I'm not pregnant," I say. But the words come out distracted because I've just caught a glimpse of myself in the mirror. I reach up and dust attic cobwebs off my head.

"Oh." She closes the stall door.

"Did you see Janet?" she asks after a moment or two.

"No."

"She looks great. Does she have a hot date or something?"

"Or something," I mutter. "I have to go."

I open the bathroom door a crack and peek out to make sure the coast is clear of Janet. Then I try Jonah's office. It's locked. And there's no answer to my knock, even though I can see lamplight coming from under the door. I wander down to the south exhibit room. Everything is beautiful. Everything is in its place.

The museum is empty. Of Jonah anyway.

A whale with an empty belly.

I walk back to the car.

"When I grow up—" I started to say to Jonz one summer day while eating an orange and sitting in the old tree at the park.

"You sound like a little kid," he interrupted. "A few hundred years ago and you'd be married already."

"Not quite," I said.

"You're fourteen," he said. "Plenty old enough."

I blushed.

He was carving a face or his initials into the tree about six inches underneath my bare toes. I sat on a low limb just above his head. My fingers smelled of orange oil after peeling the oranges we'd snuck out of his house. "Snuck" is a polite way to say "stole." They'd been in a bag marked CARO'S!!! DON'T TOUCH! Until Jonah created a "family situation."

"Right?" he asked. Then he looked up and saw my blush.

"Oh," he said. "Never mind." He carved for a bit. And I wished I wasn't a girl and didn't have to get—or not get—periods.

"So what do you want to be when you grow up?" Jonz asked. I looked down at him. He was pretending to carve, but the smile worked through. I pushed the top of his head with my foot, and he laughed.

"You're lucky you're a guy," I said.

"Oh yeah. It's just great. Basketball coaches sniffing you all over and asking you why you waste your time doing a 'faggot' thing like art. Teachers thinking you're an idiot. Girls shoving their dirty feet through your hair . . . just great."

I displayed a middle finger in sympathy.

"Come take a look at this," he said, ignoring the finger.

I dropped down from the branch and looked at the carving. He'd worked around a knot and an old scar, and somehow the knot had turned into a wrinkled face and the scar twisted down in a bearded shape.

"I like it," I said, because I didn't know how to tell him that it made me scared and warm at the same time.

He waited, and I looked at him out of the corner of my eye.

"And?" he asked.

"And what?"

He sighed. "Well, we've learned one thing. You won't grow up to be an art critic."

I snorted. "I already know what I'm going to be. I'm going to be nothing."

"Nothing?"

"I won't have time to do anything else. I'll be spending all my time keeping people from throwing you to the whales."

• • •

The museum didn't swallow Jonah.

I walk back to my car, climb in, try to think . . .

. . . and end up with my forehead on the steering wheel and being too damn close to tears for my own peace of mind.

Someone knocks on the window, and I scream.

It's Timothy.

I roll down the window.

"He's gone," Timothy says.

"Gone? You mean he quit?"

"Quit? Why would he do that? Is he going to quit? Do you know something. . . . That son of a bitch. Right before—"

"Timothy!" I say, interrupting the tirade. "I was asking *you* if he quit."

"Oh. No. He's just gone. Called me last night and said he wasn't coming in today. Said he had to go find something somewhere."

" 'Somewhere'?"

"Hole, Home . . . no, Hove," he says. "Hove. Or something like that."

Hove. Home.

Jonz and I passed each other in the fog.

"But he's probably back already," Timothy says. "He and Janet are . . ." And he makes some Monty Python winks and nudges.

"Thanks," I say.

"See you tomorrow," Timothy says.

I nod, wipe the fog of tears from my face, and roll up the car window. And that's when I remember my cell. Maybe it's because I've been in Hove for a few days, but somehow I'd forgotten the cell's existence. I can be forgiven for this. There's no point in calling Jonz. He thinks cell phones are an invasion of privacy, so he's never bothered with one.

I call India.

"I have a rental car," I say. "I need to turn it in, but I'm too tired to deal with public or ped right now."

"You sound awful," she says.

"I feel awful."

"Where are you?"

"Contemplating suicide." I remember Janet. "Or murder. I think I'm almost at the point of no return."

"Street address, you idiot."

I give her the address of the rental franchise. And then I stop by an oriental gift shop.

An hour later, the rental's turned in, and I'm holding the cigar box and sitting in India's unheated trash can of a car.

She unwraps the brown tissue paper of the new Maneki Neko cat bank and smiles. "Cute," she says.

"If it's not the same—" I begin, but she cuts me off.

"I like it."

Silence.

She taps her fingers on the steering wheel, but she doesn't put the car in gear and pull out into the mushy street. "Are you—?" she begins. *Are you all right?*

"I owe you money," I say, hoping to head the question off at the pass. I really don't want to answer a question I don't have an answer for. "Actually, my sister does."

"No, she doesn't," India says. "Well, not like you think. She left an apology, fifty bucks, and an IOU on my bed before you all left."

I stare at the woman in silk adorning the cover of the box. It feels strange to be the receptacle for so many wrong assumptions.

"The handwriting was suspiciously masculine," India says. She grins at me. "Still think he isn't daddy material?"

Okay. So my assumptions weren't so terribly far off. In the case of Geena, anyway.

"If he ever mixes genes with Geena again," I say, "they'd better buy the kid a compass."

"I'm sorry about the miscarriage," she says after we've sat in silence for a few more minutes.

"I can't find Jonz," I say, as if she's asked a question. "And I need to go to The Club."

"You think he's there?"

"I'm not going there because of Jonz."

She taps the steering wheel again. "Would this have anything to do with the guy who called?"

"Yes."

"Don't want to talk about it?"

"Virginity. Late bloomer. Needed a scalpel. Big mistake."

"Whoa!" India says. "More than I wanted to know."

"That's what I figured."

"I'm not dropping you off," she says. "I don't want to find you in the gutter, so I'm going in with you, okay? I'll go to the bathroom or something while you talk to this guy."

" 'You're a real friend,' " I say, quoting Eeyore again. " 'Not like some.' "

And even though I usually use the quote sarcastically—like when the hot dog vendor tells me I have to pay extra for jalapeños or relish—this time I mean every word.

"So you'll dedicate your life to pulling me from the whale's jaws?" Jonz asked, still laughing.

"If I don't, you'll be digested slowly and messily."

"God won't get the whale to spit me out, huh?"

"You don't believe in God."

He bowed in my direction. "Wichita Gray. Self-Appointed Savior. It has a nice ring. For a job title."

"I need a halo," I said, looking around for something yellow and suitable.

"You need blonde hair and a stained-glass window."

"Halo first."

And somehow in the middle of laughing and looking for a halo, we bumbled into each other. Jonz caught my arm to keep me from falling, and I caught the tree, and we ended up pressed against the carving of the tree spirit. The afternoon sun felt hotter, and Jonah smelled like Tide and deodorant soap and . . . Jonah. And I wanted us both to drop down into some whale's belly so we'd never fall apart and I could smell him forever.

Jonah let my arm drop. "Saviors shouldn't need saving," he said. But he wasn't laughing anymore. "You're my friend."

Call me crazy, but I've always felt like I lost my innocence the day I couldn't find a halo.

Chapter 24

It's a slow night at The Club. Surprising for a Monday. Surprising until I see that somehow, someway, Kenny has managed to slip past Mike's guard and is singing something which might be "O Sole Mio" or "She'll Be Coming Round the Mountain When She Comes." The last holdouts in the booths are either deaf or die-hard bar fiends.

"Is he really a friend of yours?" Mike asks when India and I walk into the slowly warming room. "I broke the rules when he mentioned your name."

"I work with him," I say. Then:

"Can I talk to you?"

Mike looks up and down the empty bar. "Sure. If you'll remove *it*," he gestures toward the stage and Kenny, "from the place."

For all my bluster, I'm rather shy and retiring. I'm not bouncer material. But I've had just about enough of messing up my life the last few days. Things were going so nicely, too, before India made that "joined at the hip" comment and I saw that news program.

Okay, so maybe things weren't really going so nicely, but let's just pretend for now.

I march up to the stage and yank on Kenny's jeans.

He looks down at me.

"I need a favor," I say. Yell.

The noise stops. Then it starts up again, "Wichita, sweet Wichita—"

"Kenny, please. I'm begging here. Mike won't talk to me unless you stop singing."

He stares down at me. "Why'd you do it, Wichita?" he asks in a Shakespearean kind of singsong. "Janet was sucking on him the minute you left. Why'd you let that happen? The woman's got tentacles. He doesn't stand a chance."

Did I mention that this is happening via amplifier?

Sucking?

The die-hard bar fiends—they aren't deaf, so they can hear—all turn around. No one knew The Club's open mike included improv.

Sucking?

"Kenny . . ." I say. "Please. Pretty please. I'll listen to your next audition material."

He shuts off the mike and jumps down from the stage. A collective sound of relief rises from the room.

"Promise?" Kenny asks.

"Promise." I start to walk to the bar, then I turn back to him. "What did you mean by 'sucking'?"

"Sucking. Tongues. Kissing. In the exhibit room. Whew!" He shakes his hand.

Under the Band-Aid, the cut on my thumb throbs.

"You shouldn't hurt Jonah, you know," Kenny says as we walk back toward the bar. "He loves you."

"Yeah," I say, "that's why he was sucking on Janet."

Which is all very unfair and unreasonable. I fucked the bartender, after all.

"Who's Janet?" Mike asks. "She sounds like my ex."

221

"Did your ex carry a firearm?" I ask.

Mike squints at the row of glasses hanging above his head. "Not that I recall." He nods toward a corner booth. "You wanted to talk?"

The corner booth is cold. The cracked vinyl covering the seats is cold. The draft coming in from the front windows is cold. I wrap my arms around myself to try and keep my teeth from chattering. Now that I'm here, I don't know what to say. I just know it isn't fair to leave a mess in someone else's house when you leave.

"I—" I begin.

"Is this about the other night?" Mike interrupts.

I focus on the top button of his flannel shirt. "Sort of."

"Because I don't really like these kinds of talks. They make me nervous."

Blinking—I must look like an idiot or a nocturnal animal exposed to headlights—I move my point of view from button to face. "They make me nervous, too," I say. "But I feel a little like the green scum you'd find on your grout."

"Because you took me home and . . . ah . . . ?"

"Yeah."

He nods, pursing his lips. "Not your usual style?"

"No."

"What is? Your usual style?"

I wad my fingers together and manage a shrug.

"It's the guy, isn't it?" he asks. "The one who snags all the free coffee and doesn't drink."

My heart thumps hard. "Yeah," I say again. "But I've kind of screwed it up really bad."

And it's embarrassing, but I can feel hot tears on my almost-frozen cheeks. I scrub my face on the rough coat-wool covering the crook of my arm.

"Here," Mike says, handing me a paper napkin.

"Thanks." I start shredding it between my fingers before I realize I'm sitting in front of the guy who has to pick up any stray shreds that might escape the confines of the table. "Sorry," I say, patting the napkin flat onto the table.

"Does he love you?" Mike asks.

"We've been friends since first grade."

"Wow." He says the word as if he's actually impressed. "I never tried that," he continues. "Getting it on with a friend."

"You don't 'get it on,'" I say. "You just . . . *are*, you know?"

He shakes his head.

"I don't get it either," I say. Sigh, actually. "I just . . . miss him."

Mike scratches a point between his nose and the side of his mouth. Then he holds out a hand. "Friends?" he asks.

I crunch my eyebrows down over my nose. I'm not sure—

He laughs. "No, not like that," he says. "Friends. You know—platonic. Hail-fellow-well-met. Friends."

I smile and put my cold hand into his and shake. "Friends."

India gives me an overly casual look as Mike and I walk back to the bar. She's looking for signs of misery. Maybe suicide. Even though she wouldn't actually believe someone who said I was suicidal, even if the someone was me. She knows better. But not having the gumption to actually go through with self-inflicted death doesn't mean I might not feel like death warmed over. So, like a makeup artist for the local pockmarked TV news anchor, she runs a casually critical eye over my mental state, looking for flaws in the smooth pancake surface of my face.

And I like being a starling.

Pecking, squawking, and having someone watch my back.

India is my friend. Mike is my friend. Kenny is my friend. Timothy is my friend. Janet—

Let's not take this too far.

These people are my friends. And they're here for me—peck, squawk, fight, and all. And we're part of a larger flock of people who sign their names on a soft sheet of paper in a Burger King seat. And we're part of a family larger than the few individuals who participated in our births. We're just common humanity, doing the thing that should come naturally to humanity, only sometimes it's beaten out of us under the guise of individualism. Under the guise of "supposed to." We're a flock. We might fight over that lump of bread, but when it comes to the predators of life, we're united.

No one is an individual.

Especially not me.

I'm a special part of humanity.

Because I have Jonah.

Call him a soul mate or a Siamese twin. It doesn't matter. What we had—have—is special. And I screwed it up. Now I have to fix it.

But fixing it means I have to see him. And as soon as he finds the cache in the Hove house empty, he's going to come home. If I'm in his apartment—

"Wanna help me do a little B&E?" I ask India.

Mike rolls his eyes up to the row of glasses again. "I didn't hear that," he says.

"I did," Kenny says.

"Where?" India asks.

I slug down the last of Kenny's beer. "Jonz' place."

"Finally," India says.

Amen.

We are not merely a collection of DNA. We are a collection of memories. Our memories determine who we are, what we think, our reactions to stress, fear, pain, joy, love, sex. . . . And unlike the collections that pass through the museum, a memory collection is a fluid, ever-changing thing. Memories are never static. And since I'm nothing more or less than the combined whole of my memories, I'm a fluid, ever changing being. Not static. I could no more cut Jonah and me apart than I could cut off my own head. We're joined at the brain because we have the same memories. But like the Siamese twins who are forever joined, we're not the same person.

We're just indispensable to each other.

I can fix this.

I can fix this.

I hope.

"What are you *doing?*" India hisses in my ear. Behind her, Mike and Kenny jockey for a good view of my efforts. When I asked India if she wanted to help, I must have sounded like someone issuing a group invitation. Mike closed the bar, and he and Kenny climbed into the back seat of India's car. *"We can help,"* Kenny said when India and I stared at them.

"I'm trying to use a credit card to open the door," I say. "What's it look like?"

"Push harder," Mike says, reaching over India's shoulder to wave his finger at the doorjamb. "You have to bend the card a little."

"Thanks," I say. "I couldn't have done this without your help."

We're standing in the hall of Jonah's apartment building. It's a nasty hole of a building. Too run-down to be considered artsy-shabby by the Lake Forest hipsters. The walls and hallway are suspiciously stained. Anyone looking at the place would think the museum doesn't pay a living wage. Okay, it doesn't. But Jonah stays *here* because the other tenants have a live-and-let-live attitude. Lord knows, no one is peering out and calling the cops on four idiots trying to break into one of the apartments.

Kenny leans in. "This is like a bad movie," he says in a loud whisper. "Any minute now he's going to—"

I nearly fall into Jonah's stomach.

"—open the door," Kenny finishes.

I stand up. "Hi," I say to Jonz.

"Bye," Kenny says to no one in particular. And being his helpful best, he takes off back down the building's hall and escapes down the stairs. At the foot of the stairs, he starts singing something that sounds like "Love Me Tender." An apartment door bangs open. A woman screams.

India and Mike are made of sterner stuff than Kenny the Coward.

For about five seconds.

"Well, looks like everything's cool," India says. "See you later, Wichita. Jonz."

Mike coughs. "Yup, real cool. See ya."

Then he and India scoot off after Kenny.

"Do you like coffee?" I hear Mike ask as their footsteps fade down the building stairs.

"Hi," Jonz says to me. He looks down at the credit card in my hand. "Is it maxed out?"

I put my hands behind my back. "Something like that."

"Because opening doors messes up the magnetic strip."

I nod. I had some little "I'm so sorry" speech that I mentally wrote and memorized on the drive over here, only . . . only when Jonah opened the door, everything came tumbling down like the walls of Jericho.

"I thought you wanted away from me," Jonz says, "but here you are trying to break into my apartment." He catches the top edge of his door in one hand, long fingers wrapping over the stained wood.

I look at his fingers. Remember the merry-go-round. *Come on. Trust me.*

"You could have knocked," he says.

"Would you have let me in?"

He looks at me. "I think so."

"Jonah?" a voice I barely recognize asks. "Who is it?"

Janet. Trying to sound sexy.

Or suckable.

"Just someone trying to sell me an alarm system," Jonz says over his shoulder.

I bend down and pick up the cigar box that I set on the floor during my unhappy career as a burglar. "Here," I say. "You can have this free of charge. I could have saved you a trip to Hove."

And I *shove* the box into his stomach.

Chapter 25

I almost leave.

Almost.

Have you ever read those books that are all about regrets? About the heroine who should have stood her ground and fought for happiness but didn't? I almost end the rest of my days writing regretful memoirs. Because I'm scared and embarrassed, and Jonz is looking at me with that foreign smile on his face that he never gives me.

Almost.

But two steps away from the door I remember my mother living with my father. How if she'd only grown a backbone and gotten over her fear and pride and all those "supposed tos," she might have lived the rest of her life with Jared LiaKos. And Jonah and I would be brother and sister. Or maybe we wouldn't exist at all.

Only we do.

And I am not my mother.

I will not make the mistakes of my parents.

Our parents.

I twirl around, take the two steps back to Jonah's door—he's still watching me and trying to catch his breath from the surprise cigar box attack—and I push past him and on into the apartment.

"Come on in," he says.

Janet is sitting on the futon couch. She's in fire-engine red. A tropical exotic. And totally out of place.

"Hi," I say.

"Hi, Wichita. Are you the one trying to sell an alarm system?"

"Do you have your own car?" I ask.

She blinks. "Y-yes."

"Would you mind driving yourself home? I know this is really rude and all, but I have to talk to Jonz."

It is rude. But less rude than wrapping my fingers around her throat and throttling her.

She stares at me. At Jonah. Then she folds her arms across her chest and gives me a "you've been shoplifting in the cookie aisle" look.

It doesn't go with the red dress at all.

"This is highly unusual," she says in her best rent-a-cop voice. One hand starts to slip down for her holster, only—lucky me—she isn't packing today.

"I'm sorry," I say, holding up her coat. "I'll walk you down."

"No, thanks. I can find my way out." She stands up and takes the coat from my outstretched fingers. At the door she turns around. "I sort of wondered, you know, if it was really over between you two." She smiles at Jonz and shakes the tin cows in her ears. "If it doesn't work out, you can always call me."

"Thanks," he says.

I mutter something and shut the door behind her red bouncing-pom-pom butt. I really can't stand red pom-poms, even if they turn out to have enough personality to see through Filthy Jeff's earwax.

But once the door is closed, I'm at a loss. All the bravado is as damaged as the magnetic strip on my credit card. Jonz is still standing where I pushed him when I forced my way into the apartment. He looks down at the cigar box and traces the outline of the overblown beauty with one finger. His black hair hangs over his forehead, and I can't see his face.

It doesn't matter.

I can hear the brush of his finger on the cardboard.

The sound drags down my spine and makes me want to weep. I open my mouth to say I'm sorry and that I'll leave.

"I saw your mother today," he says.

I shut my mouth. "Why?"

He looks up, pushes the hair out of his eyes, and smiles before setting the box down on the table. "She asked me the same thing. Said I should be somewhere else."

And with that cryptic comment, he flops down on the futon couch and kicks off his shoes. I sit down on the floor. Because I'm too tired to find a chair.

I wonder if the scalpel severed our brain waves. Like a cake knife cutting through a double-layer chocolate cake at the church potluck. I can't *hear* Jonz. Panic and double-layer sorrow sucks me down, and I say the first absurd thing that comes into my head.

"I'm sorry I messed up your date."

Not that I still don't feel like spitting on Janet's shoes. Sucking. Huh.

Silence.

I look up, and Jonah is frowning at me. In a kind of confused way. "That was a date?" he asks.

"Wasn't it?"

"She knocked. I opened the door. For all I knew, she had a gun in that little purse, so I let her in. More like a mugging than a date."

"She didn't ask—?"

He shakes his head, interrupting me. "It was my fault," he says. "I kissed her the day you left. Right after you left."

"Oh."

"Oh." He reaches out and plays with the fringe of the old afghan he wrapped me up in the night I nearly froze to death in the snow. "What about Mike?" he asks.

I'm staring at the fringe and Jonz' fingers. "Mike?"

He gives a rueful half laugh. "I'm sorry," he says. "Maybe I jumped to conclusions that night. I thought you and he . . ." He trails off.

I swallow. "In the case of Mike, you'd be right. We . . ." I make some kind of movement with my hand. "We . . . I . . . I jumped the poor guy."

"Ah."

The inhaled sound grates on my spine even worse than his finger on the cardboard face. "Yes, 'ah.' And what about Morgan?"

The skin around his eyes scrunches up. "Morgan?"

"Green Volvo. Red pom-poms. Perky . . ." I hold both hands in front of my chest. "Morgan."

"Morgan."

"Morgan."

"That's digging up some history."

"Uh-huh." I fold my arms across my body until I realize I probably look a lot like Janet when I do that.

"Guilty," he says.

"No shit," I say. "I saw you."

"You didn't need to see me," he says. "I told you about it. I didn't try to hide it."

"I didn't say you did."

"You made it sound like I did."

"Did not."

"Did to."

"Did not."

He grabs a fistful of his hair in one hand and drops his head onto the back of the couch. "What are we arguing about?"

"You and Morgan."

"No," he says. "You and Mike."

"No."

"Yes."

I start laughing at the exact same moment as I realize Jonah's shoulders are shaking so hard he can barely get a breath.

The smile dies in his eyes. He leans forward and catches my wrist in one hand.

"Morgan was sex," he says. "I was horny, seventeen—"

"Sixteen," I interrupt.

"—sixteen, then."

"Mike was a scalpel," I say. "To cut us—you and me—apart."

"Remind me to ask you about that one," he says. "I still don't get it."

"Don't bother."

I can hear his thumb brush over the skin that covers my veins. I can hear the brush a split second after I feel it. The sound is delayed, like the pounding of a hammer from a distant construction site. The hard hat's hammer falls without a sound. As he raises the hammer again, you hear the *thuck* of metal on wood. I feel skin pressed to skin. Then the brush finds my ears. Jonah's eyes are black holes in the blanket over the sky, and I'm falling. . . .

Friends forever.

I breathe and break my fall into eternity. "I . . ." Another breath.

"Thank you for getting the cigar box," he says, so soft I almost miss it.

"If I'd known you were going down there for it—"

He squeezes my wrist, and I look back up into the future of forever.

"I didn't go to Hove for the box," he says. "I don't need what's in that box to remember. I went back for you."

I reach up with my free hand to brush his hair away from where it's fallen across his cheek. "Do you still need saving?" I ask. "Because I have job experience. At being a savior."

He smiles and his cheek moves under my fingertips. "Where's your halo?"

"Right here."

His lips are warm under mine.

Outside the window, in the cedar trees, a sleepy starling wakes up long enough to mutter a song to the birds beside him. Then he tucks his head back under a dark wing and goes to sleep.

Separation Anxiety

Karen Brichoux

A CONVERSATION WITH KAREN BRICHOUX

Q. Separation Anxiety *takes place in both the present and in the past via the heroine's memories. Why did you decide to structure the book this way?*

A. A person's memory is a devious thing. Take any event shared by two or more people and you will find that none of them remembers the event the same way. But what happens to a person's opinions—and their vision of the world that has been shaped by those opinions—when their memories turn out to be different from reality? Wichita has memories of her childhood that have shaped her current opinions about her family, Jonah, and the world, but now she's confronted by the discovery that her memories may not contain the whole story.

I wanted the reader to experience Wichita's memories through *her* eyes while also being able to see what she was unable to see. At the same time, I wanted the reader to begin to understand Wichita's family and Jonah—their motives, emotions, and beliefs—without ever having to leave Wichita's head. In some cases, this makes Wichita an unreliable narrator—what she says and thinks and remembers may not be the truth—but I wanted the story to be about *her* journey to understanding herself, her family, and her relationship with

Jonah. The best way to do this seemed—to me, anyway—to use a simultaneous presentation of past and present.

Q. Your first book, Coffee & Kung Fu, *was about a woman in her twenties who is on the brink of discovering herself.* Separation Anxiety *has a similar theme. Is there something about this time in a woman's life that fascinates you? Or is it just coincidence?*

A. I don't think it's coincidence. Our lives are made up of a series of crossroads. Each one of us is cruising happily along on the straight and narrow, then we reach a fork in the road where we have to make a decision. Paper or plastic? Mayo or mustard? Should I marry him or not? Should I have kids or not? Should I keep working at this dead-end job or pack my bags and move to Hong Kong? Should I break off this friendship forever or just go on pretending there's nothing wrong? These kinds of decisions are part of the human experience. Some decisions we choose to make, and some are forced upon us. Sometimes we make the right decision, and sometimes we make the worst decision of all. At this point in my life, I enjoy focusing on the crossroads that come up for women in their twenties and thirties. Fifteen or twenty years from now, I'll probably be more interested in choices that confront women in their forties and fifties.

Q. You grew up in the Philippines as a daughter of American missionaries. What kind of impact do you think this has had on your writing?

A. I think the one element in my writing that comes from my childhood is my focus on navigating the river of social relationships. When you do a lot of hopping from one country to another—crossing the boundaries of language and culture— you spend most of your time trying to figure out what the person across from you is really saying. Body language, facial expressions, gestures—these things become more important than the words coming out of someone's mouth. I think the tension created by two people trying to communicate is at the heart of everything I write, and that tension is probably a direct result of my childhood experiences.

Q. What do you think is the hardest part about being a published author?

A. I think it's different for every author, but for me, the hardest part actually has *two* parts. First, seeing my work commercialized (reduced to a single catchy sentence for marketing purposes); and second, trying not to fall into the trap of writing for someone other than myself. Every person on this planet has something important to say. (Ultimately, it may only be important to *them*, but they will still try to communicate that importance to other people.) Every person has their own unique experiences that create their vision of the world. Using *my* unique experiences, I try to write about things that I think are important and that convey my vision of the world. And I hope like crazy that I will be able to connect with readers and have at least a few of them think, "I know *exactly* what she means." But if I try to write *to* the readers, I end up writing about talking toasters. And believe me, no one wants to know what my toaster says to me in the mornings before I've had my coffee. . . .

QUESTIONS FOR DISCUSSION

❖

1. *Separation Anxiety* focuses on what it means to be a family. As a child, Wichita comes to the conclusion that memories are thicker than blood and that Jonah is her family. What do you think is the defining characteristic of family? Is it shared memories, shared experiences, or something else?

2. Because she was afraid they would become involved in a sexual relationship, Wichita's mother tried to break up Wichita and Jonah's friendship when they were teenagers. Are American parents too focused on this particular "sin"? Does society repress sexuality to the point that it becomes an obsession rather than just a normal part of being human?

3. Why do Wichita's parents stay together? Wichita thinks it's because no one else can "absorb all the anger they have to give." Do you agree with her? Or is the situation more complex than it seems?

4. Wichita wants to make her mark on the world and leave some impression behind to show that she existed in a certain time and place. Do you have this need, too? Where do you think the need comes from? Is it part of being human or is it culturally driven?

5. In chapter 24, Wichita says, "No one is an individual." American society is supposedly built on the theory of individualism, but when you look at the world around you, do you think this is true? Should it be true?

Karen Brichoux lives in the Midwestern United States with her spouse, four cats, and a large dog who suffers from debilitating separation anxiety. She is also the author of *Coffee & Kung Fu*, and invites readers to drop by her Web site at www.karenbrichoux.com.